The Harry Potter QUIZ BOOK

Buster
Books

First published in Great Britain in 2004 by Buster Books,
an imprint of Michael O'Mara Books Limited
9 Lion Yard
Tremadoc Road
London SW4 7NQ

A CIP catalogue record for this book is available from the British
Library.

ISBN 1-904613-51-9

1 3 5 7 9 10 8 6 4 2

Written by Guy Macdonald
Illustrated by Geo Parkin
Edited by Samantha Barnes
Printed and bound by Bookmarque Ltd, Croydon, Surrey

How to play

Answer the questions in any order you choose – perhaps you are a specialist on one particular subject or book. Here's how the questions work...

Question number   Question

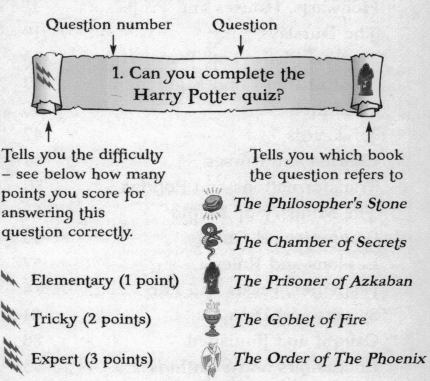

1. Can you complete the Harry Potter quiz?

Tells you the difficulty – see below how many points you score for answering this question correctly.

Tells you which book the question refers to

The Philosopher's Stone

The Chamber of Secrets

Elementary (1 point)   *The Prisoner of Azkaban*

Tricky (2 points)   *The Goblet of Fire*

Expert (3 points)   *The Order of The Phoenix*

If you choose to play for points, you may award half points for half-correct answers. You do not have to give exactly the same words written in the answers at the back of the book; e.g. if an answer is written as 'Professor McGonagall' you would still be correct to say only 'McGonagall'.
Have fun and have your wits and wands ready.

Contents

Harry, Ron and Hermione

1. What colour are Harry's eyes?

2. In which month is Hermione's birthday?

3. Who of Harry, Hermione and Ron are made prefects?

4. Who partners Hermione at the Yule Ball?

5. From what type of tree is Harry's wand made?

6. How many brothers and sisters does Ron have?

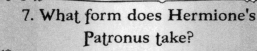

7. What form does Hermione's Patronus take?

8. What curse did Harry survive aged one?

9. What Quidditch team does Ron support?

10. What are the names of Harry's deceased parents?

11. What was Harry's first racing broomstick?

12. What type of broomstick does Ron have in his first four years at Hogwarts?

13. What shape is the scar on Harry's forehead?

14. What is Hermione's last name?

15. When were Harry's parents killed: Christmas Day, Halloween or Harry's first birthday?

16. How many Weasleys are at Hogwarts during Ron's second year?

17. What is the form of Harry's Patronus?

18. What does Hermione score in her end-of-first-year Charms exam: 99%, 100% or 112%?

19. Who of Harry, Ron and Hermione can see the winged Thestrals?

20. What colour is Hermione's cat?

21. What colour jumper does Ron get from his mother every Christmas?

22. Whom does Harry turn into after drinking Polyjuice Potion: Crabbe or Goyle?

23. What sort of snake does Harry release from the zoo?

24. From which parent does Harry get his eye colour?

25. What are the names of Ron's parents?

26. Who sends Harry his first owl post at Hogwarts: Mrs Weasley, Dumbledore or Hagrid?

27. Which of Ron's brothers was first to be head boy?

28. What was Harry's mother's maiden name?

29. Which of Ron's brothers was a Quidditch Captain?

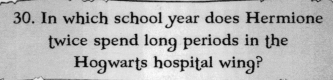

30. In which school year does Hermione twice spend long periods in the Hogwarts hospital wing?

31. Does Hermione have one or two Muggle parents?

32. What is the name of Harry's godfather?

33. Who is Ron's youngest brother or sister?

34. What name does Ron give the owl that he is given by Sirius Black?

35. In what country does Hermione spend her summer holidays before her third year?

36. What is Ron's, Harry's and Hermione's favourite drink in Hogsmeade?

37. Ron's wand contains the hair of what magical creature?

38. What is the name of Ron's family's house?

39. How many hands does the Weasley's kitchen clock have: one, two or nine?

40. What shape does Hermione's Boggart take?

41. What does Harry break in his second-year Quidditch match against Slytherin: his leg, his arm or his glasses?

42. What date is Harry's birthday?

43. Other than Gryffindor, in which House does the Sorting Hat think Harry would do well?

44. Whose pleading voice does Harry hear in his head when Dementors appear?

45. Who is the cause of Harry's 'secret heartache', according to Rita Skeeter's article in *Witch Weekly*?

46. What is the name of the village where Ron's family live?

47. What was the name of Harry's parents' house?

48. Ron's pet rat, Scabbers, used to belong to which of his brothers?

49. Which Muggle school was Harry expected to attend?

50. According to Lord Voldemort, which of Harry's parents died first?

51. Which of Harry's arms is pierced by the venomous fang of the Basilisk?

52. Who first uttered the prophecy about Harry and Lord Voldemort?

53. The prophecy about Harry and Lord Voldemort might equally have applied to which other boy?

54. Does Hermione compare Ron's emotional range to a teaspoon, a gargoyle or a wart?

55. What is the name that Dobby uses for Ron Weasley?

56. Who rescued Harry from the ruins of Godric's Hollow?

57. On which birthday is Harry upset not to receive any cards from his Hogwarts friends?

58. Whose birthday does Harry usually spend with Mrs Figg?

59. Where do Harry, Ron and Hermione spend Christmas in the fifth year?

60. What colour hair do the Weasleys have?

61. In which Hogwarts House were Ron's mother and father?

62. The song of what bird gives Harry hope in his graveyard duel with Lord Voldemort?

Hogwarts, Houses and Professors

63. What are the four school Houses?

64. Name three of the four animals that feature on the Hogwarts coat of arms.

65. On what date does the school year start?

66. How many tables are in the Great Hall?

67. What is the first line of the school song?

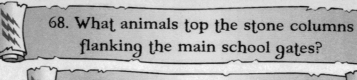 68. What animals top the stone columns flanking the main school gates?

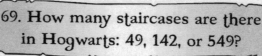 69. How many staircases are there in Hogwarts: 49, 142, or 549?

 70. Who has a long crooked nose, blue eyes and wears half-moon spectacles?

 71. What animal represents Hufflepuff on the Hogwarts coat of arms?

 72. Who is Keeper of Keys and Grounds?

 73. Bold, Fair, Sweet, Shrewd – match each of these four virtues with its corresponding House, as sung by the Sorting Hat.

 74. Who teaches flying lessons?

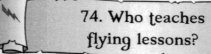 75. What animal can Professor McGonagall turn into?

 76. What subject does Hagrid teach?

 77. What shape is Dumbledore's office: round, square or star-shaped?

12

78. What subject does Professor Trelawney teach?

79. In Harry's third year, who teaches Defence Against the Dark Arts?

80. Who is the Defence Against the Dark Arts teacher in Harry's fourth year?

 81. Which professor is Head of Hufflepuff?

82. What is Hagrid's first name?

83. What is the village near Hogwarts that third-years are at times permitted to visit?

84. On what level of Hogwarts is the Slytherin common room?

 85. Whose classroom smells of garlic?

 86. Which teacher has a wooden leg?

87. At Harry's careers consultation, which teacher strongly supports his ambition to become an Auror?

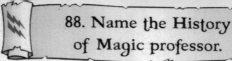

88. Name the History of Magic professor.

89. Whom does Dumbledore appoint as the new Divinations teacher after Professor Trelawney's dismissal?

90. In what room can the portraits of Everard and Dilys be found?

91. What does Professor Quirrell wear on his head?

92. Who teaches about werewolves in Defence Against the Dark Arts?

93. How many governors of Hogwarts are there?

94. Who gives Harry special lessons in Occlumency?

95. Who taught Care of Magical Creatures before Hagrid?

96. What is the name of the boisterous tree on the Hogwarts lawn?

97. Complete the name of the librarian: Madam...

98. In whose empty classroom is Harry permitted to practise spells at lunchtimes for the third Triwizard task?

99. How long has Professor McGonagall been teaching at Hogwarts by Harry's fifth year: 39, 59 or 99 years?

100. In which tower is the Owlery situated: North, South, East or West?

101. The Fat Lady guards the hidden entrance to the common room of which House?

102. What springs to life to reveal the staircase leading to the Headmaster's office?

103. Who was Head of Hogwarts during Tom Riddle's era: Dedalus Diggle, Armando Dippet or Nicolas Flamel?

104. Complete the name of the statue guarding the prefects' bathroom: Boris the...

105. What subject would Professor Snape really like to teach?

106. The tapestry of Barnabas the Barmy hangs opposite the entrance to which room?

107. What is Professor Moody's nickname?

108. What does the sign say on the door to Moaning Myrtle's bathroom?

109. Complete the name of the matron: Madam...

110. What is Filch the caretaker's first name?

111. On Harry's very first day at Hogwarts, who stands up to say the words 'Nitwit! Blubber! Oddment! Tweak!'?

112. What is the name of the knight who stands in for the Fat Lady at the hidden entrance to Gryffindor Tower?

113. Where in Hogwarts is the Goblet of Fire placed to receive applications for the Triwizard Tournament?

114. In which House was Dumbledore when he was a Hogwarts student?

115. Who takes over as Head of Hogwarts during Dumbledore's suspension?

116. Which House wins the House Championship in Harry's third year?

117. What colour is Professor Moody's mad eye?

118. Who tops up their magic with a Kwikspell course?

119. Professor Umbridge teaches what subject?

120. Prior to Harry's arrival at Hogwarts, for how many years in a row had Slytherin won the House Championship: 6, 16 or 60?

121. Who is Deputy Head of Hogwarts?

122. Which Hogwarts professor is a werewolf?

123. On what floor is the Gryffindor common room?

124. Name the very first student in Harry's first year to be Sorted by the Sorting Hat.

125. What is the name of Hagrid's half-brother?

126. What shape is Harry's dormitory: square, triangular or circular?

127. Who temporarily replaces Hagrid as Care of Magical Creatures teacher?

128. How many beds are in Harry's dormitory?

129. What relation of Dumbledore is the wizard Aberforth: brother, cousin or father?

130. To keep his Occlumency lessons secret, what must Harry pretend he is studying?

131. A one-eyed statue of what guards the entrance to the secret tunnel to Honeydukes?

132. Roughly how many house-elves work in the Hogwarts kitchens according to Nearly Headless Nick: 1,000, 500 or 100?

133. What is the name of the dark wizard defeated by Dumbledore in 1945?

134. What ancient sporting event is held at Hogwarts after more than a hundred years' lapse?

135. Whose first names are Helga, Godric, Rowena and Salazar?

136. What popular Muggle sport does Dumbledore enjoy, according to his Chocolate Frog card?

137. Which is the only school House not to suffer attacks by the Basilisk?

138. What is the name of the resident poltergeist?

139. Whom does this describe: a thin woman, draped in shawls and glittering beads?

The Dursleys

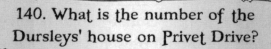

140. What is the number of the Dursleys' house on Privet Drive?

141. On which birthday does Harry receive a pair of old socks and a coat-hanger from the Dursleys?

142. What sort of dogs does Aunt Marge breed in her large country house?

143. What is Mr Dursley's newspaper of choice?

144. What does Dudley throw out of his bedroom window in a tantrum: some doughnuts, his PlayStation or Harry's wand?

145. In what village do the Dursleys live?

146. Which resident of number four, Privet Drive receives a Howler?

147. What is the name of Mr Dursley's company?

148. Dudley's secondary-school uniform consists of a maroon tailcoat and orange knickerbockers. Name one other item.

149. What do the Dursleys buy Dudley as a welcome-home present at the start of the summer holidays?

150. What does Mr Dursley's company make?

151. Aunt Marge brings a dog to number four, Privet Drive. What is its name?

152. Whom does Mr Dursley ask to dinner in the hope of landing the biggest deal of his career?

153. What is the name of Mr Dursley's old school?

154. Complete the full name of Harry's Squib neighbour: Arabella Doreen...

155. Who phones Privet Drive to speak to Harry, sending Mr Dursley into a fume?

156. What should cats definitely not be able to do, according to Mr Dursley?

157. To what hotel does Mr Dursley take the family to escape the deluge of letters for Harry?

158. What attacks Dudley and Harry in the alleyway between Magnolia Crescent and Wisteria Walk?

159. What sport does Dudley take up at Smeltings?

160. Do the Dursleys have a real fire or an electric fire in their living room?

161. Complete the name of the institution that Aunt Marge thinks Harry attends: St Brutus's Secure Centre for Incurably...

162. How many presents does Dudley eventually receive on his tenth birthday: 36, 37 or 39?

163. Who has a cat called Mr Tibbles?

164. How many owls visit the Dursleys' after the attack of the Dementors: 5, 50 or 500?

165. In what county do the Dursleys live?

166. What explodes in Aunt Marge's hand during lunch at the Dursleys?

167. What is Mrs Dursley's first name?

168. What is the name of Dudley's best friend?

169. Who has a sister called Marge: Mr or Mrs Dursley?

170. Who is Big D?

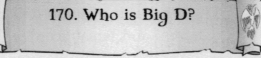
171. What is wrong with Mrs Figg on Dudley's 11th birthday?

172. Where does Harry send Hedwig during Aunt Marge's visit?

Magical Places and Transport

173. What is the name of the bookshop in Diagon Alley?

174. What is the name of the wizarding bank?

175. What is the name of the emergency transport for stranded witches or wizards?

176. From which platform of King's Cross station does the Hogwarts Express leave?

177. At what time does the Hogwarts Express leave for the new school year at Hogwarts?

178. What is the name of the wand shop in Diagon Alley?

179. What sort of shop do Gambol and Japes keep?

180. Number twelve, Grimmauld Place is the headquarters of which secret society?

181. What is the name of the only entirely non-Muggle settlement in Britain?

182. What London station does Harry use to return from Diagon Alley to Privet Drive?

183. What is the short name of the wizarding hospital?

184. What is the name of the wizarding prison?

185. Name all four forms of magical transportation officially available to witches and wizards.

186. Where does Madam Rosmerta work: The Three Broomsticks, Honeydukes or Zonko's?

187. By what mode of transport do the Weasleys travel to fetch Harry for the Quidditch World Cup?

188. Where does Neville Longbottom go to visit his parents?

189. What are wizarding doctors called?

190. In what county do the Malfoys live: Devon, Surrey or Wiltshire?

191. What sort of shop is Honeydukes: a patisserie, an ice-cream parlour or a sweetshop?

192. What colour is the emergency wizarding bus?

193. What is the name of the joke shop in Hogsmeade?

194. Where does Fleur Delacour find work after leaving Beauxbatons?

195. To what do the initials WWN refer?

196. What are the two other big European schools of wizardry apart from Hogwarts?

197. What is the name of the northern terminus of the Hogwarts Express?

198. In which disreputable inn was the prophecy about Harry and Lord Voldemort first spoken?

199. What is the name of the most haunted dwelling in Britain?

200. By what means of transport do the Advance Guard escort Harry from the Dursleys' to Grimmauld Place?

201. What is the name of the hill from which Harry, Hermione and the Weasleys travel to the World Cup?

202. What is contained in Gringotts vault 713?

203. What is Fred and George's joke shop in Diagon Alley going to be called?

204. How does Harry travel to Diagon Alley to stock up for his second year at Hogwarts?

205. What is the name of the shabby pub that stands at the entrance of Diagon Alley?

206. How does the Durmstrang delegation travel to Hogwarts?

207. What is the name of the resident house-elf at Grimmauld Place?

208. In what country does Bill Weasley work for Gringotts as a curse breaker?

209. Phineas Nigellus, a former Head of Hogwarts and ancestor of Sirius Black, can move between portraits in which two places?

210. Which Muggle department store fronts St Mungo's: Rhodes & Higgs Ltd, Loach & Webber Ltd or Purge & Dowse Ltd?

211. What magical objects are well suited to transporting large groups of wizards from one spot to another at a prearranged time?

212. Where in Hogsmeade do Cho Chang and Harry go for coffee on Valentine's Day?

213. Where do you find a shop called Dervish and Banges: Hogsmeade or Diagon Alley?

214. In what county does the inventor of the Philosopher's Stone live?

215. Does a wizard need a licence to Apparate?

216. Who shuts the enchanted barrier to platform nine and three quarters so that Harry and Ron miss the Hogwarts Express?

217. On Harry's first visit to Gringotts, what is the name of the goblin that guides him to his parents' vault?

218. Whose portrait screams obscenities in the hallway of Grimmauld Place?

219. What form of transport meets all but the first-years off the Hogwarts Express?

220. How do Harry, Hermione and the Weasleys travel to King's Cross at the start of Harry's fourth year at Hogwarts?

221. How do Harry and Mr Weasley travel to Harry's disciplinary hearing at the Ministry of Magic?

222. What is the first name of the barman of The Leaky Cauldron?

223. Is Hogwarts north, south, east or west of London?

224. What sin is warned against on the doors of Gringotts?

225. What form of magical vehicle is banned in Britain by the Registry of Proscribed Charmable Objects?

226. How many Ministry cars take Harry, Hermione and the Weasleys to King's Cross station?

227. How many golden Galleons does Harry see in the Weasley's vault at Gringotts: 1, 100 or 1,000?

228. Where does Harry spend the last two weeks of his summer holidays before his third year at Hogwarts?

229. What is sold in Florean Fortescue's shop?

230. What colour is the Hogwarts Express?

231. Whose family tree is on a tapestry in Grimmauld Place?

232. How do Harry and Ron get to Hogwarts at the start of their second year?

233. On the back of which Hippogriff does Sirius Black escape from Hogwarts?

234. In which family's home is there a secret chamber hidden under the drawing-room floor?

235. By what form of transport do Harry and his friends travel to the Ministry to save Sirius Black?

236. Do Harry and Ron become uncomfortably hot or uncomfortably cold in the flying Ford Anglia?

Magical Items and Equipment

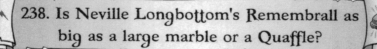

237. Out of what material is the Goblet of Fire made?

238. Is Neville Longbottom's Remembrall as big as a large marble or a Quaffle?

239. What gift from Egypt does Ron give Harry for his 13th birthday?

240. What is the name of the stone basin in which Dumbledore stores thoughts?

241. In what harmless-looking item does Hagrid keep his broken wand?

242. What does Dudley eat that makes his tongue swell?

243. In view of his friends, what is Neville Longbottom given by his mother in St Mungo's?

244. What is the name of the Dark detector in which Professor Moody sees his enemies?

245. For Christmas in his fourth year, who gives Harry a penknife that can unlock any lock and undo any knot?

246. On what sort of racing broom did Madam Hooch learn to fly?

247. How many locks are there on Professor Moody's trunk: five, seven or ten?

248. Lord Voldemort's and Harry's wands both contain a feather from which phoenix?

249. Who receives an envelope full of Bobutuber pus at breakfast?

250. What does Harry use to pacify the three-headed dog, Fluffy?

251. What type of sweet do Fred and George Weasley try out on first-years in the Gryffindor common room?

252. What two items does Professor Lupin return to Harry before leaving Hogwarts?

253. Fleur Delacour's wand contains a hair from the head of what?

254. What does Harry throw into Goyle's cauldron to divert Professor Snape's attention during Potions?

255. How many Sickles are there in a Galleon?

256. Viktor Krum's hornbeam wand contains the heartstring of what creature?

257. What is the name of the device used by Dumbledore to extinguish the street lamps on Privet Drive?

258. Where would you find an Invisibility Booster?

259. What flavour beans does Bertie Bott make?

260. What jewelry does Bill wear that causes Mrs Weasley some concern?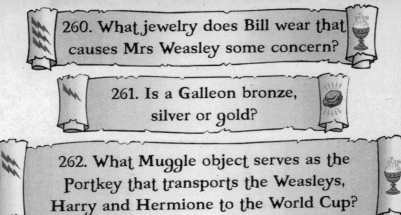

261. Is a Galleon bronze, silver or gold?

262. What Muggle object serves as the Portkey that transports the Weasleys, Harry and Hermione to the World Cup?

263. How many Knuts make one Sickle: 9, 19 or 29?

264. What sort of gold vanishes after a few hours?

265. What sort of quill does Rita Skeeter use to interview Harry?

266. How many sets of work robes are first-years instructed to bring to Hogwarts?

267. From what tree was Harry's mother's wand made?

268. What type of repellent does Hagrid say he is looking for on Knockturn Alley?

269. What does Ron use to mend his broken wand?

270. How long was Hagrid's wand: 12, 14 or 16 inches?

271. From what tree was Lord Voldemort's wand made?

272. How much does Harry's wand cost: 7 Sickles, 7 Galleons or 70 Galleons?

273. What magazine does Luna Lovegood read upside down on the Hogwarts Express?

274. What is the form of the Portkey that Harry, Hermione and the Weasleys use to get back from the World Cup?

275. What is the name of Neville Longbottom's hideous-looking plant that erupts on the Hogwarts Express?

276. What does Harry use to get a closer look at the World Cup final?

277. What does the inscription on the Mirror of Erised mean – 'Erised stra ehru oyt ube cafru oyt on wohsi'?

278. What piece of Muggle equipment saves Colin Creevey from the Basilisk?

279. What state-of-the-art broomstick does Harry see in Quality Quidditch Supplies during his stay at The Leaky Cauldron?

280. How many times must a teacup be swilled around to make a reading?

281. In what magical object does Harry desperately hope to see the face of his dead godfather?

282. Ron buys a new wand for his fifth year. How long is it: 11, 14 or 18 inches?

283. What device does Professor McGonagall give to Hermione to help her take extra lessons in her third year?

284. With what item does Hermione try to find hidden words in Tom Riddle's diary?

285. What colour is the Philosopher's Stone?

286. On the Weasley's grandfather clock, what is written where the figure 12 would normally be: 'Home', 'Work' or 'Mortal Peril'?

287. What object holds the power of eternal life?

Quiddit ch

288. In which position do Fred and George Weasley play?

289. How many players are there on each side?

290. In what colour robes do Gryffindor play?

291. What colour are the Bludgers?

292. What are the three players called whose job it is to score?

293. In what colour robes do Hufflepuff play?

294. What is the name of the Gryffindor Captain and Keeper during Harry's first three years at Hogwarts?

295. What type of broomstick does Lucius Malfoy give to all seven members of the Slytherin team?

36

296. How many golden poles with hoops stand at either end of the Quidditch pitch?

297. Which ball is red and about the size of a football?

298. What type of broomstick do Fred and George Weasley fly?

299. In what month does the Quidditch season begin?

300. How many points is the Golden Snitch worth?

301. What broomstick can accelerate from 0 to 150 miles an hour in 10 seconds?

302. How many ways are there of committing a foul: 200, 500 or 700?

303. What colour is the strip of Ron's favourite team, the Chudley Cannons?

304. Which players have the role of blocking the Bludgers?

305. Who catches the Golden Snitch in Harry's third-year match against Hufflepuff?

306. What enchanted object attacks Harry in his second-year match against Slytherin?

307. Who is Harry's opposite number in his third-year match against Ravenclaw?

308. Who is Harry pleased to see watching his first-year match against Hufflepuff?

309. How many years ago did Britain last host the World Cup: 3, 30 or 300 years?

310. How many balls are used in a Quidditch game?

311. In which position does Gilderoy Lockhart say he used to play?

312. What country knocked England out of the World Cup?

313. What country plays Bulgaria in the World Cup final?

314. Who cast the spell that broke Harry's fall in a match versus Hufflepuff?

315. Which teams are about to play when Professor McGonagall orders all students back to their common rooms?

316. What is the name of Fred Weasley's and George Weasley's friend who likes to commentate at Quidditch matches?

317. Name five of the seven Gryffindor players who defeat Slytherin to win back the Quidditch Cup after seven years.

318. Who gives Harry an 'ear-bashing' for failing to attend the Keeper tryouts in his fifth year?

319. Who is the commentator for the World Cup final?

320. What colour are Bulgaria's flying robes?

321. For what team did Ludo Bagman play in his days as a Beater?

322. How many Gryffindors tryout to become the new Keeper after Oliver Wood?

323. Who replaces Harry as Gryffindor Seeker after his ban by Professor Umbridge?

324. Who wins the World Cup?

325. Watching Harry's first ever Quidditch game, his friends wave a banner. What is written on it?

326. What is the name of the Ravenclaw Seeker who has supported the Tornados since the age of six?

327. What is the name of the diversion tactic that the Bulgarian Seeker so expertly pulls off?

328. What is the name of Bulgaria's star player?

329. What position does Alicia Spinnet play for Gryffindor?

330. Which two Houses are scheduled to play the first Quidditch match of every season?

331. How many spectators does the World Cup stadium seat: 1,000, 10,000 or 100,000?

332. Who becomes Gryffindor Captain after Oliver Wood?

333. What slogan is written on the Slytherin badges for Ron's first game?

334. How many goals does Ron concede in his first match against Slytherin?

335. What team is Oliver Wood signed to play for after leaving Hogwarts?

336. How many goals does Ron concede in his second match: 3, 9 or 14?

337. Which House inflicts on Gryffindor its worst defeat in 300 years at the end of Harry's first season?

338. To what institution does Lucius Malfoy give a large donation in order to get tickets for the Top Box at the World Cup final?

339. Which Gryffindor supports the Kenmare Kestrels?

340. How many feet off the ground do the Quidditch goal hoops stand?

341. Who is Oliver Wood's successor as Gryffindor Keeper?

342. Which family sits behind Mr Weasley in the Top Box at the World Cup final?

343. Who catches the Golden Snitch in the World Cup final?

344. What position do Crabbe and Goyle play for Slytherin?

345. What is the technical term for 'excessive use of elbows'?

Triwizards

346. Name the impartial selector of the champions chosen to compete in the Tournament.

347. Did the Tournament originally take place every four, five or six years?

348. On the night of which seasonal feast are the names of the champions revealed?

349. How much prize money does the winner of the Tournament receive?

350. How many tasks do the champions face in the Tournament?

351. In what month do the delegations from Beauxbatons and Durmstrang arrive at Hogwarts?

352. What colour robes do Durmstrang wear under their furs?

353. What two items appear crossed on the Beauxbatons coat of arms?

354. With which House do the Durmstrang delegation sit at the Welcome Feast?

355. Where is the clue for the second task hidden?

356. Give the surnames of the five judges of the Tournament.

357. What is the name of the Headmistress in charge of the Beauxbatons delegation?

358. What anti-Harry message flashes on the Slytherin badges during the Tournament?

359. What is the name of the Headteacher of Durmstrang?

360. Which challenge does Cedric Diggory win: the first, second or third?

361. Which two Ministry officials join the staff table at the Welcome Feast?

362. Which champion is third to enter the dragon enclosure?

363. Which champion gets the golden egg from the dragon in the quickest time?

364. Towards the end of what month does the final task take place?

365. Which Diagon Alley shopkeeper comes to check the wands at the start of the Tournament?

Charms and Curses

366. What spell does Hermione unwillingly use on Neville Longbottom on their way to rescue the Philosopher's Stone?

367. What curse does Harry manage to throw off in Professor Moody's lesson?

368. What magic word does Harry use to get Tom Riddle's diary back from Draco Malfoy?

369. What magic word produces a Summoning Charm?

370. McGonagall, Dumbledore, Snape and which three other professors place enchantments around the Philosopher's Stone?

371. What curse does Madame Maxime use on two giants and Victor Krum use on a dragon?

372. What does the magic word 'Scourgify' do: clean, tidy or pack trunks?

373. Who attacks Cedric Diggory with the Cruciatus curse in the maze?

374. What charm did medieval witches use to protect themselves from flames?

375. Hermione uses what magic word to keep the rain off Harry's glasses in the Hufflepuff versus Gryffindor Quidditch match?

376. What magic word produces instant flames?

377. What magic words conjure a Patronus?

378. Mentioning which curse upsets Neville Longbottom in Professor Moody's lesson?

379. What sort of charm does Harry use on Draco Malfoy in Duelling Club?

380. On whom are Ron and Hermione going to use the Leg Locker curse in Harry's first-year Quidditch game against Hufflepuff?

381. What magic word illuminates the tip of a wand?

382. What magic word is the best defence against a Boggart?

383. What type of charm backfires on Gilderoy Lockhart in the Chamber of Secrets?

384. What curse does Harry throw at Bellatrix Lestrange in the Atrium of the Ministry?

385. What magic words make objects fly?

386. What type of charm makes Hagrid's pumpkins reach enormous sizes?

387. What magic word produces a Memory Charm?

388. Does the magic word 'Colloportus!' seal or open doors?

389. What magic word revives the victim of a Stunning Charm?

390. What type of charm does Professor Moody think tricked the Goblet of Fire into selecting four champions instead of three?

391. What curse causes its victim to lose free will?

392. What is the name of the charm involving the magical concealment of a secret inside a Secret-Keeper?

393. What curse kills its victim?

394. What magic words does Harry use to paralyse his enemies in the Department of Mysteries?

395. What magic words reveal the last spell that a wand has performed?

396. In his Occlumency lessons Harry blocks Professor Snape with what type of charm?

397. What is the Jinx that slows down or obstructs attackers?

398. What type of charm does Harry use to get the golden egg?

399. What magic word produces a Tickling Charm?

400. What colour jets of light from the wands of Lord Voldemort and Harry clash in the graveyard?

401. In Duelling Club, Professor Snape uses the magic word 'Expelliarmus!' to disarm whom?

402. Who yells 'STUBEFY!' to no effect in the Department of Mysteries?

403. According to Professor McGonagall, which are trickiest to vanish: mammals or invertebrates?

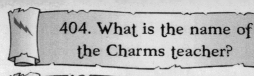

404. What is the name of the Charms teacher?

405. Name the three Unforgivable Curses.

406. What charm do Fleur Delacour and Cedric Diggory use to swim under water?

407. What does the magic word 'MORSMORDRE' conjure?

408. What is the name of the charm that makes you feel happy?

409. What type of spells do the dragon-keepers use to pacify the Hungarian Horntail after its long journey to Hogwarts?

410. What magic word produces a Shield Charm?

411. What charm renders Harry virtually invisible on his night flight to Grimmauld Place?

412. What type of charm triggers the letter to Harry from the Improper Use of Magic Office during the summer holidays?

413. What charm is Harry taught to use to fend off the Dementors?

414. What does the victim of the Cruciatus curse experience?

415. With what spell does Harry disable the Blast-Ended Skrewt in the Triwizard maze?

416. What curse kills Cedric Diggory?

417. A hex causes what word to appear in spots across Marietta Edgecombe's face?

418. Whose unconscious body is brought back to school through a secret tunnel with the help of the magic word *Mobilicorpus*?

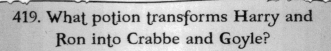

Transformations and Potions

419. What potion transforms Harry and Ron into Crabbe and Goyle?

420. What do Fred and George Weasley call their range of sweets that cause sickness?

421. In the form of what sort of animal does Professor McGonagall first appear?

422. Hermione attempts to transform into which Slytherin girl?

423. What type of animal does Peter Pettigrew become?

424. What bewildering brew does Harry concoct for his third-year Potions exam?

425. What appears on Fred and George Weasley's faces after crossing the Age Line?

426. How many poison bottles are among the potions guarding the Philosopher's Stone?

427. Which of these ingredients is needed to make Strengthening Solution: salamander blood or pomegranate juice?

428. In Harry's first ever Transfiguration lesson, what does Professor McGonagall turn her desk into?

429. What potion does Professor Lupin take at the full moon: Wolfsbane Potion, Moonstone Potion or Leg Locker Potion?

430. What is the name of the substance that Harry swallows to breathe under water?

431. What is the name for witches or wizards who transform at will into animals?

432. What is the name for a witch or wizard who can change appearance at will?

433. In what tasty food does Hermione put the Sleeping Draught for Crabbe and Goyle?

434. Asphodel and wormwood make what sort of potion: sleeping, cheering or tickling?

435. In the stomach of what animal might you find a bezoar stone?

436. What small animal does Harry turn into a snuffbox for his first-year Transfiguration practical exam?

437. What plant returns transfigured or cursed victims to their original state?

438. Who feeds Shrinking Solution to Neville Longbottom's toad, Trevor?

439. The pus of what plant cures acne?

440. How many registered Animagi are in Hermione's library book: 7, 70 or 700?

441. What potion includes the ingredients Bicorn horn and Boomslang skin?

442. What shape does Neville Longbottom's Boggart take?

443. What can Rita Skeeter turn into at will?

444. Harry loses how many points in his first Potions lesson with Snape: 2, 20 or 50?

445. What is the name of the Truth Potion with which Professor Snape threatens Harry?

446. How long do Harry and Ron spend as the living replicas of Crabbe and Goyle: 10 minutes, 1 hour or 2 hours?

447. Which noise does Professor McGonagall make as she transforms: a pop, a crack or a thwap?

448. How many drops of Ageing Potion do Fred and George Weasey take to trick the Goblet of Fire: one, four or the whole bottle?

449. In Professor Lupin's lesson in the staff room, who steps forward to finish off the Boggart: Neville Longbottom, Harry or Ron?

450. What shape does Parvati Patil's Boggart take?

451. What potion is Harry given by Madam Pomfrey to regrow the bones in his arm?

452. What does Professor Lupin's Boggart briefly become before disappearing?

453. Into what sort of animal does Professor Moody turn Draco Malfoy in the dinner queue?

454. How long does Veritaserum Potion take to mature, according to Snape: a day, a month or a year?

455. Are Monkshood and Wolfsbane derived from an animal, a vegetable or a mineral?

456. Name the healing potion that Madam Pomfrey gives to people with colds.

457. Which teacher enchanted the chessboard protecting the Philosopher's Stone?

The Ministry of Magic

458. Who is the Minister for Magic?

459. Which former Quidditch star heads the Department of Magical Games and Sports?

460. What Muggle object serves as the visitors' entrance to the Ministry?

461. How are inter-departmental memos delivered in the Ministry?

462. What is the correct Muggle word for Amos Diggory's 'please-men'?

463. What are the white objects floating in the tank in the Department of Mysteries?

464. What law helps protect Muggles from dark wizardry?

465. Which Ministry official speaks over 200 different languages?

466. What Muggle disturbance is Mr Weasley sent to investigate in Bethnal Green?

467. Who lodges an official complaint about Buckbeak to the Committee for the Disposal of Dangerous Creatures?

468. What silver letter do the Wizengamot wear on their plum-coloured robes?

469. What sort of hat does the Minister for Magic wear on official Ministry business?

470. In what country is Ministry worker Bertha Jorkins when she goes missing?

471. What is the name for Ministry workers attached to the Department of Mysteries?

472. What are set at regular intervals into the Atrium walls at the Ministry?

473. On what level of the Ministry is the Department of Mysteries?

474. What number must be dialled at the visitors' entrance to the Ministry?

475. By what name does Dumbledore refer to Lord Voldemort in the Atrium?

476. In which Ministry department do Bode and Croaker work?

477. Which senior Ministry official mysteriously fails to show in the Top Box at the World Cup Final?

478. What name is Percy Weasley mistakenly called by his head of department?

479. Complete the name of the Ministry office in which Mr Weasley works: The Misuse of...

480. With which Ministry office are Animagi legally required to register?

481. Which Ministry worker is criticized in the *Daily Prophet* over the Ministry's handling of the World Cup?

482. What is the name of the Ministry official who sent Sirius Black to Azkaban without trial?

483. In the Ministry's Prophecy Room, which Death Eater cautions Bellatrix Lestrange not to attack Harry?

484. What is the name of the female interrogator at Harry's hearing who resembles a large toad?

485. Which member of the Order of the Phoenix is arrested at 1a.m. in the Ministry?

486. Does Cornelius Fudge vote to convict or clear Harry of all charges at his hearing?

487. Which Ministry worker do Harry, Ron and Hermione come upon in the woods after the World Cup final?

488. Who was the Minister for Magic before Cornelius Fudge: Armando Dippet, Millicent Bagnold or Barty Crouch (Snr)?

489. Barty Crouch (Snr) staggers out of the Forbidden Forest into which two Triwizard champions?

490. What is Percy Weasley's function during Harry's disciplinary hearing?

491. What is the name of the Death Eater who mimics Harry in a mock baby voice in the Hall of Prophecy?

492. Complete the sentence: Percy lands his first job in the Department of International Magical...

493. Whom does Harry see whispering with the Minister for Magic on Level Nine just after his hearing?

494. What is the name of Mr Weasley's assistant?

495. Does Harry expect to find Sirius Black in row 19, 57 or 97 in the Hall of Prophecy?

496. What is the name of the watchwizard at the Ministry?

497. Who is afraid that Dumbledore is raising a private army at Hogwarts to take on the Ministry?

498. Which of these Ministry workers is in the Order: Amos Diggory, Kingsley Shacklebolt or Madam Bones?

499. Which senior Ministry official is a witness to the execution of Buckbeak?

500. Where in the Ministry is the Fountain of Magical Brethren situated?

501. What reward is the Ministry offering for the capture of Sirius Black: 1,000 or 10,000 Galleons?

502. Which Ministry department is summoned to Privet Drive to deflate Aunt Marge?

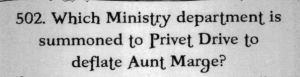

Creatures and Ghosts

503. Nearly Headless Nick is the resident ghost of which House?

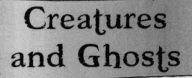

504. What sort of pet has Hagrid wanted since he was a child?

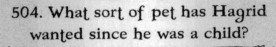

505. What is the name of the lizards that like a good bonfire?

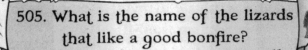

506. What sound does Dobby make when he apparates out of the Dursleys' kitchen: a pop, a crack or a bang?

507. What creatures flutter around the Great Hall during the Halloween feast?

508. What sort of animal is Norbert?

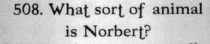

509. In which room does Professor Lupin's Defence Against the Dark Arts class confront the Boggart?

510. What alcoholic spirit do the Beauxbatons horses drink?

511. The Hungarian Horntail and Chinese Fireball are breeds of what?

512. Which little bearded creatures are mascots for the Irish national team at the World Cup?

513. What sort of dog does Hagrid have?

514. Who is the Slytherin ghost?

515. What is the name of Dumbledore's pet bird?

516. In which country will Norbert live on leaving Hogwarts?

517. What is the name of the creature that can shape-shift into your worst nightmare?

518. What is the largest creature in Hogwarts lake?

519. The heads of what creatures decorate the stairway of Grimmauld Place?

520. What monster lurks within the Chamber of Secrets?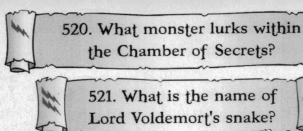

521. What is the name of Lord Voldemort's snake?

522. What creatures are excellent at finding hidden treasure?

523. Dumbledore discovered how many uses for dragon's blood: 9, 12 or 21?

524. What is the name of the one-legged creature that lures travellers into bogs?

525. What is the colour of unicorn blood?

526. What sort of creature is Aragog?

527. What sort of owl does Draco Malfoy have: tawny, screech or eagle?

528. What creature grabs Harry's ankles as he swims to the bottom of the lake?

529. Which dragon does Cedric Diggory face: a Hungarian Horntail or a Swedish Short-Snout?

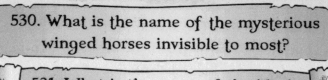

530. What is the name of the mysterious winged horses invisible to most?

531. What is the name of the black-bodied and bearded centaur?

532. What is the name of Barty Crouch (Snr)'s house-elf?

533. Name the ghost that haunts the girls' toilet.

534. How many years has Nearly Headless Nick been dead at his Deathday Party in Harry's second year: 50, 250 or 500?

535. What is the name of the three-headed dog guarding the Philosopher's Stone?

536. What is the name of Hagrid's dog?

537. How many giants are in the world, according to Hagrid: 80, 180 or 800?

538. Who is Errol?

539. What giant creature do Harry and Cedric Diggory repel in the Triwizard maze?

63

540. What is the name of the centaur that saves Harry from the hooded figure in the forest?

541. For what sole purpose are the tiny Scops owls used by Hogsmeade Post Office?

542. Is Hedwig a male or female owl?

543. What is the name of the household pests in the curtains at Grimmauld Place?

544. Who, more than anyone, scares the poltergeist, Peeves?

545. What is the first creature that Harry meets in the Triwizard maze?

546. What happens to you if you hear the cry of a fully grown Mandrake?

547. What does Hagrid mix with brandy to feed Norbert every half-hour: Boomslang skin, chicken blood or pomegranate juice?

548. What is the name of the owl that lands unconscious on Harry's bed on his 13th birthday?

549. What is the native
language of goblins?

550. From the egg of what creature
is the Basilisk said to hatch?

551. What sort of animal is Lavender
Brown's pet, Binky?

552. What colour are the
Beauxbatons horses?

553. Which dragon does Fleur Delacour face:
a Chinese Fireball or a Welsh Green?

554. What highly suspicious hedgehog-like
creature goes beserk if offered milk:
a Knarl, a Niffler or a Bowtruckle?

555. What creature is depicted on the front
doorknocker of Grimmauld Place?

556. What is the full name
of Nearly Headless Nick?

557. The Thestrals are attracted
by the smell of what?

558. What creature do Harry and Ron
vanquish in the girls' toilet?

559. What tiny creatures cause pandemonium in Professor Lockhart's first Defence Against the Dark Arts lesson?

560. Where would you find Red Caps: wherever there has been bloodshed, in watery places, or in dark spaces?

561. What colour is a unicorn foal?

562. What is the name of the tree-guardians that usually live in wand-trees?

563. Name a type of dragon still living in the wild in Britain.

564. From which book is the name Hedwig taken: *A History of Magic*, *The Monster Book of Monsters* or *Magical Me*?

565. What creature does Aragog fear above all others?

566. What sort of creature is Dobby?

567. What is the name of Percy Weasley's screech owl?

568. To which House did the Fat Friar belong when he was alive?

569. What sort of creature is a cross between a horse and an eagle?

570. What is the name of the 10-foot-long creature with an exploding tail that attacks Harry in the Triwizard maze?

571. What colour do unicorn foals turn when they are about two years old?

572. What is the name of the animal summoned before the Committee for the Disposal of Dangerous Creatures?

573. What sound is fatal to the Basilisk?

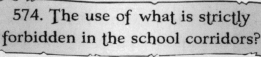

Lessons and Rules

574. The use of what is strictly forbidden in the school corridors?

575. What does a grade 'A' stand for?

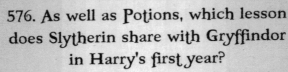

576. As well as Potions, which lesson does Slytherin share with Gryffindor in Harry's first year?

577. What does SPEW stand for?

578. Which three animals are first-years allowed at Hogwarts?

579. At what age are witches and wizards permitted to use magic out of school?

580. In what type of buildings do first-years take Herbology lessons?

581. At the top of which tower is Professor Trelawney's classroom: North Tower, South Tower or Owl Tower?

582. What does Neville Longbottom break on his first flying attempt: his broomstick, his wrist or his Remembrall?

583. According to Sirius Black, were he and James Potter Hogwarts prefects?

584. What does a grade 'D' stand for?

585. In which class does Ernie Macmillan apologize to Harry for calling him Slytherin's heir?

586. From what time are students confined to their Houses during Dumbledore's suspension from Hogwarts?

587. Who gets injured in Hagrid's first Care of Magical Creatures lesson?

588. How many points do Harry, Ron and Hermione get in total for defeating the troll?

589. Dumbledore redesigns Firenze's classroom to look like what?

590. In what lesson does Harry dream about the Riddle House for the second time?

591. What is the name of the ancient science concerned with the making of the Philosopher's Stone?

592. What type of magic seals the mind against magical intrusion?

593. With which House do Gryffindors take Herbology in Harry's second year?

594. What prestigious wizarding award does Professor Snape win, and then lose, for his part in the bungled capture of Sirius Black?

595. What is the minimum age for entrants to the Tournament?

596. What does NEWT stand for?

597. Which two new subjects does Harry take in his third year?

598. Which three Gryffindors get a lifelong Quidditch ban from Professor Umbridge?

599. What is the name for the magical power to steal the feelings and memories from another person's mind?

600. What does the author Cassandra Vablatsky promise to unfog?

601. In which lesson is Harry when he sees spiders heading for the Forbidden Forest?

602. What does Harry produce for an extra point in his OWL Defence Against the Dark Arts practical?

603. What career does Professor Moody urge Harry to consider?

604. What subject does Hermione dramatically quit in her third year?

605. How many Sickles does Hermione charge for joining SPEW: one, two or three?

606. Which two teachers spar in the first demonstration of the Duelling Club?

607. What subject did Dumbledore teach during Tom Riddle's day?

608. What is the latest time that fifth-years are allowed in the Hogwarts corridors?

609. What position at Hogwarts is created by the passing of the Educational Decree Number 23?

610. What magical security system is placed around the Goblet of Fire to prevent under-age students entering the Tournament?

611. What exam are Harry, Hermione and Ron taking when they see Hagrid attacked by Professor Umbridge's Ministry cronies?

612. What is the title of Gilderoy Lockhart's autobiography?

613. What does OWL stand for?

614. What does a grade 'E' stand for?

615. What is the name for someone with no magic powers but born to a wizarding family?

616. What is the name of Professor Umbridge's gang of student thugs?

617. Which two Gryffindor girls are especially fond of Divination?

618. Is Phyllida Spore the author of *Magical Theory* or *One Thousand Magical Herbs and Fungi*?

619. Griselda Marchbanks is head of which wizarding authority: Examinations, Wireless or Transport?

620. How long is Ron's homework on 'The Medieval Assembly of European Wizards' meant to be: 1 foot, 3 feet or 5 feet?

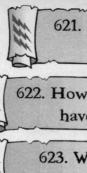

621. How many OWLs did Bill and Percy Weasley each get?

622. How many times does Charlie Weasley have to take his Apparition test?

623. What is the minimum number of NEWTs needed to become an Auror?

624. Does Hermione appoint Ron treasurer or secretary of SPEW?

625. Is Quentin Trimble the author of *The Dark Forces: A Guide to Self-Protection* or *Fantastic Beasts and Where to Find Them*?

626. Seen by Harry and Ron from under the Invisibility Cloak, what does Lucius Malfoy give Dumbledore in Hagrid's hut?

627. In what classroom does Professor Lupin give Harry Anti-Dementor lessons?

628. Do students normally need to show mastery of Conjuring Spells at OWL level, or at NEWT level?

629. Whose application is rejected by the Headless Hunt on a technicality?

630. What must Harry make turn cartwheels in his OWL Charms practical?

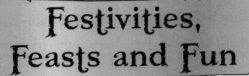

Festivities, Feasts and Fun

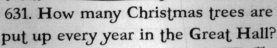

631. How many Christmas trees are put up every year in the Great Hall?

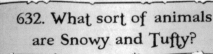

632. What sort of animals are Snowy and Tufty?

633. Dumbledore doesn't like Bertie Bott's Every Flavour Beans because he once ate one of which flavour?

634. What is the name of the musical act at the Yule Ball?

635. What sort of cake does Hagrid give Harry for his 11th birthday?

636. On what feast day do Hermione and Ron take their first trip to Hogsmeade?

637. For his first Christmas at Hogwarts Harry gets a box of handmade fudge from Mrs Weasley. What else does she send him?

638. Is Colin Creevey's Muggle father a postman, a milkman or a bus driver?

639. When Harry is a second-year, which two first-years are his greatest fans?

640. What is the name of Percy Weasley's girlfriend in Ravenclaw?

641. Who is first to enter the Great Hall for the Sorting Ceremony, Harry or Ron?

642. Give the first names of Harry's four Gryffindor room-mates.

643. Ron's owl brings Harry a parcel for his 13th birthday containing a birthday card, a present, a letter and what else?

644. Who gets Harry's Triwizard winnings?

645. How many Valentine cards does Gilderoy Lockhart say he received: 26, 34 or 46?

646. Who gives Harry *The Monster Book of Monsters* for his 13th birthday?

647. What is the name of Parvati Patil's twin sister in Ravenclaw?

648. Which two other first-years join Harry and Ron on their boat trip to Hogwarts?

649. In their second year, as Harry and Ron watch the first-year Sorting Ceremony, who is standing directly behind them?

650. It costs Harry 11 Sickles to get to London on the Knight Bus, but what would he get in addition for another two Sickles?

651. What type of Muggle object does Mr Weasley collect besides batteries?

652. What is the command used to wipe the Marauder's Map clean?

653. What Muggle sweet is Dumbledore particularly fond of?

654. Whom does Harry take to the Yule Ball: Hermione Granger, Cho Chang or Parvati Patil?

655. In what room does Harry receive a wet kiss from Cho Chang?

656. Who gives Harry a *Broomstick Servicing Kit* for his 13th birthday?

657. Which Gryffindor Chaser partners Fred Weasley at the Yule Ball?

658. What practical but dull Christmas present does Harry get from Hermione in OWL year?

659. 'GALLONS OF GALLEONS!' Who advertises part-time paid work on the Gryffindor noticeboard?

660. Which of Seamus Finnigan's parents is a Muggle?

661. What is the Sloth Grip Roll: an Unforgivable Curse, one of Mrs Weasley's puddings or a Quidditch move?

662. Fred and George Weasley bet on which team to win the World Cup?

663. To whom is Mr Weasley referring when he uses the word 'pumbles'?

664. How many birthday cakes does Harry receive on his 14th birthday?

665. In his fourth year, what item of clothing does Harry give to Dobby for Christmas?

666. When Ron is a first-year, in which country do his parents spend Christmas?

667. What colour is Hermione's Yule Ball dress?

668. In her fifth year, what does Hermione give to Kreacher for Christmas?

669. What small dental item do the Dursleys give Harry for Christmas in his second year at Hogwarts?

670. Who is Neville Longbottom's second choice of partner for the Yule Ball?

671. What game do the Headless Hunt play at Nearly Headless Nick's Deathday Party?

672. What household furniture do Bill and Charlie spar with above the Weasley lawn?

673. Which teacher makes a surprising last-minute entrance to the Christmas feast in Harry's third year?

674. What is the name of the *Daily Prophet* reporter who covers the Tournament?

675. Whom does Ron ask to the Yule Ball, and get a silent shrug-off?

676. Who is Ginny Weasley's boyfriend after Michael Corner?

677. Which Gryffindor interrupts Professor Snape's Potions lesson to bring Harry out for the Wand Weighing ceremony?

678. Which Gryffindor boy supports West Ham?

679. Whom does Rita Skeeter call 'an obsolete dingbat' in her article about the International Confederation of Wizards' Conference?

680. Which Gryffindor sets Nifflers loose in Professor Umbridge's office?

681. Who is first to cross the Age Line: Fred or George Weasley?

682. Who gives Harry a brand-new Firebolt racing broomstick for Christmas?

683. How many times has Gilderoy Lockhart won the *Witch Weekly* Most-Charming-Smile Award: 5, 10 or 25?

684. Who is looking at Harry when he wakes up on Christmas Day in his fourth year?

685. What sort of racing broomstick does Ron get for becoming a prefect?

686. Which Ministry worker takes the place of Barty Crouch (Snr) on the top table at the Yule Ball?

687. Whom does Cedric Diggory take to the Yule Ball?

688. How many Galleons do the Weasleys win in the *Daily Prophet* Grand Prize Galleon Draw: 700, 800 or 900?

689. Who is Michael Corner's girlfriend after Ginny Weasley?

690. Who drops a water bomb on Ron's head as he enters the Entrance Hall in his fourth year at Hogwarts?

691. Who intercepts Harry's post during the summer holidays before his second year?

692. What brand of whisky does Mr Weasley pour into his wife's tea to calm her nerves?

693. In which country does Luna Lovegood hope to find a Crumple-Horned Snorkack during her summer holidays?

694. Who sends Harry a musical Valentine?

695. According to Luna Lovegood, do Heliopaths inhabit air, fire or water?

696. In which country do Mr and Mrs Weasley spend Christmas in Ron's second year at Hogwarts?

Secrets and Danger
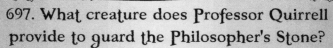

697. What creature does Professor Quirrell provide to guard the Philosopher's Stone?

698. Where does Harry hide his personal belongings from the Dursleys?

699. What is Hagrid seeking on his top-secret mission for Dumbledore?

700. What sort of creature attacks Mr Weasley in the Ministry?

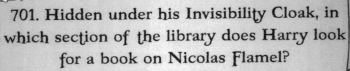

701. Hidden under his Invisibility Cloak, in which section of the library does Harry look for a book on Nicolas Flamel?

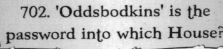

702. 'Oddsbodkins' is the password into which House?

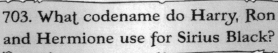

703. What codename do Harry, Ron and Hermione use for Sirius Black?

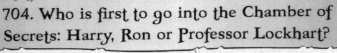

704. Who is first to go into the Chamber of Secrets: Harry, Ron or Professor Lockhart?

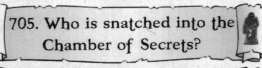

705. Who is snatched into the Chamber of Secrets?

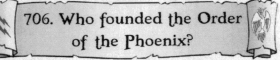

706. Who founded the Order of the Phoenix?

707. In what room does Draco Malfoy agree to fight Harry in a duel, then fail to show?

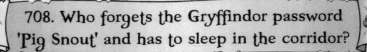

708. Who forgets the Gryffindor password 'Pig Snout' and has to sleep in the corridor?

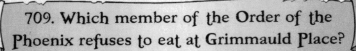

709. Which member of the Order of the Phoenix refuses to eat at Grimmauld Place?

710. 'Thanksss, amigo.' Where is Harry when he hears these words?

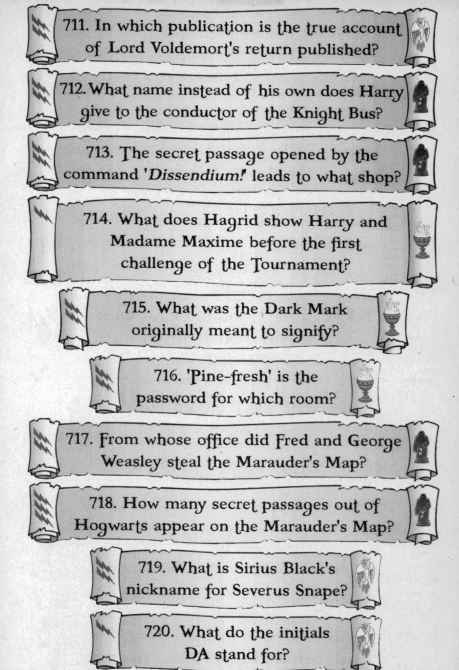

711. In which publication is the true account of Lord Voldemort's return published?

712. What name instead of his own does Harry give to the conductor of the Knight Bus?

713. The secret passage opened by the command '*Dissendium!*' leads to what shop?

714. What does Hagrid show Harry and Madame Maxime before the first challenge of the Tournament?

715. What was the Dark Mark originally meant to signify?

716. 'Pine-fresh' is the password for which room?

717. From whose office did Fred and George Weasley steal the Marauder's Map?

718. How many secret passages out of Hogwarts appear on the Marauder's Map?

719. What is Sirius Black's nickname for Severus Snape?

720. What do the initials DA stand for?

721. How long had Peter Pettigrew been spying on Harry's parents before their deaths: a week, a month or a year?

722. From whom is Harry trying to escape when he backs into the room containing the Mirror of Erised?

723. Who tells Harry what to do when the wand-connection with Lord Voldemort breaks in the graveyard?

724. With whose unwitting assistance does Sirius Black get into Gryffindor Tower?

725. What was Professor Lupin's nickname when he was at Hogwarts?

726. Who is Gurg?

727. Who tells Harry that the Dark Lord's servant is about to rejoin his master?

728. Who tried to kill the school boy Severus Snape by guiding him to the werewolf in the Shrieking Shack?

729. Who warns Harry not to return to Hogwarts in his second year?

730. Who is heard to mutter 'He's at Hogwarts' in his sleep?

731. How many consecutive nights does Harry visit the Mirror of Erised?

732. In what room is Harry when he first hears the ice-cold voice of the snake?

733. Who is Secret-Keeper for the Order of the Phoenix?

734. Who fulfils Professor Trelawney's prophecy: 'Around Easter, one of our number will leave us for ever'?

735. Who stole the passwords from Gryffindor Tower to help Sirius Black?

736. Which teacher sneaks into the Shrieking Shack under Harry's Invisibility Cloak?

737. Padfoot, Wormtail and Prongs are all illegal what?

738. What is the name of the language that Harry uses to talk to snakes?

739. Who sends Ron a night-time note to warn him not to stay friends with Harry?

740. What fruit does Hermione tickle to gain entrance to the kitchens?

741. Who lets slip that Professor Lupin is a werewolf, leading to his resignation?

742. What password gets Harry and Ron into Slytherin disguised as Crabbe and Goyle?

743. What is the worst term of abuse for someone born to a Muggle family?

744. On what date in Tom Riddle's diary does Harry discover Hagrid's secret: June 13, January 30 or July 13?

745. Who sits next to Winky in the Top Box of the World Cup under an Invisibility Cloak?

746. What is the number of Sirius Black's vault at Gringotts: 711, 117 or 717?

747. Which two members of the Order escort Harry, Hermione and the Weasleys back to Hogwarts on the Knight Bus?

748. Harry, Ginny Weasley and Neville Longbottom are transfixed by what in the Department of Mysteries?

749. What is the name of the illegal club whose members are bound to secrecy by a confidentiality agreement?

750. Where is Ron when Harry and Hermione smuggle Norbert out of Hogwarts from the highest tower?

751. Who runs into the Forbidden Forest when Sirius Black is captured by the Dementors at Hogwarts?

752. Where does the secret tunnel under the Whomping Willow emerge?

753. Where does Barty Crouch (Jnr) keep the real Professor Moody hidden?

754. What does Harry hear on the other side of the veil in the Department of Mysteries?

755. When Willy Widdershins eavesdrops in the Hog's Head, is he disguised as a witch or hidden under dirty bandages?

Caught and Punished

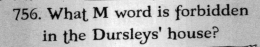

756. What M word is forbidden in the Dursleys' house?

757. Whose idea is it to travel to Hogwarts by flying car, Harry's or Ron's?

758. How many years did Sirius Black spend in Azkaban?

759. For the use of what charm is Harry expelled from Hogwarts shortly before his fifth year?

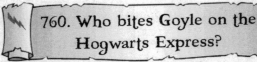

760. Who bites Goyle on the Hogwarts Express?

761. In his week-long detention with Professor Umbridge, with what is Harry made to write his lines instead of ink?

762. Which teacher confiscates Harry's new Firebolt in the Gryffindor common room?

763. Who does Hagrid threaten in the Forbidden Forest for insulting Dumbledore?

764. Who offends the centaurs by calling them half-breeds in the Forbidden Forest?

765. Which tedious household chore must Ron, Fred and George do in punishment for flying Mr Weasley's car?

766. How does Barty Crouch (Snr) punish Winky's behaviour at the World Cup?

767. In which number courtroom is Harry's disciplinary hearing: one, two or ten?

768. In which department of the Ministry does Harry's hearing take place?

769. Which wizarding newspaper reports the incident of the flying Ford Anglia?

770. Which two Gryffindors does Professor McGonagall summon into her office before the feast at the start of Harry's third year?

771. What is the name for a Dark-wizard-catcher?

772. After Hagrid is suspected of opening the Chamber of Secrets for a second time, where does Cornelius Fudge send him?

773. In which month is Harry's disciplinary hearing at the Ministry?

774. Who catches Harry, Ron and Hermione coming out of Moaning Myrtle's toilet, taking five points from Gryffindor?

775. What form of punishment is inadvertently carried out on Barty Crouch (Jnr) after the Tournament?

776. Which Order member is admitted to the Creature-Induced Injuries ward of St Mungo's?

777. How many members of the Magical Law Enforcement Patrol did it take to arrest Sirius Black and take him to Azkaban: 4, 10 or 20?

778. Where at number four, Privet Drive does Mr Dursley keep Harry's magical possessions under lock and key?

779. Who is exposed as the sneak in Dumbledore's Army?

780. In whose office do Harry and Ron miss the welcome feast in their second year?

781. Who is responsible for the regurgitating Muggle toilets: the dark wizard Grindelwald, Willy Widdershins or Lucius Malfoy?

782. Who provides Harry's defence at his disciplinary hearing?

783. In coming to Hogwarts by flying car, Harry and Ron flout the Decree for the Restriction of what?

784. In whose office is Sirius Black locked awaiting the Dementors?

785. Which Gryffindor stays in the dormitory alone while the others celebrate Harry's selection as Triwizard champion?

786. Which Weasley attacks Draco Malfoy after beating Slytherin at Quidditch for the fifth year running?

787. In which part of Hogwarts does Hermione finally catch Rita Skeeter?

788. What should Harry and Ron have done, according to Professor McGonagall, when they missed the Hogwarts Express?

789. Peter Pettigrew is escorted from the Shrieking Shack between which two people?

790. What is the name of the Auror who wipes Marietta Edgecombe's memory?

791. What is the name of the rat whom Crookshanks has it in for?

792. What part of the Basilisk's body does Fawkes attack?

793. Which two teachers can see Harry even when he is wearing his Invisibility Cloak?

794. At what time does Professor McGonagall stop the Gryffindor party after their sensational victory against Ravenclaw?

795. Who is the tall wizard with long, auburn hair that briefly apprehends Tom Riddle in the Entrance Hall?

796. What does Ron get from Mrs Weasley after arriving at Hogwarts by flying car?

797. How long is Harry's detention after his first class with Professor Umbridge?

Encounters and Sightings

798. Harry and Draco Malfoy stumble upon which dead creature in the Forbidden Forest?

799. What does Professor Trelawney see in Harry's tea leaves?

800. In which shop in Diagon Alley does Harry first meet Draco Malfoy?

801. In his fifth year at Hogwarts, Harry sees whom attacking Mr Weasley in a dream?

802. Which Ministry worker's head appears in the Weasleys' fire?

803. Harry finds Ron behind which statue before the Keeper trials: Lachlan the Lanky, Merlin the Moron or Wilfred the Wistful?

804. In what Muggle street does Harry first spot the black dog?

805. Who is the shabbily-dressed wizard that Ron, Harry and Hermione find sleeping in the last carriage of the Hogwarts Express?

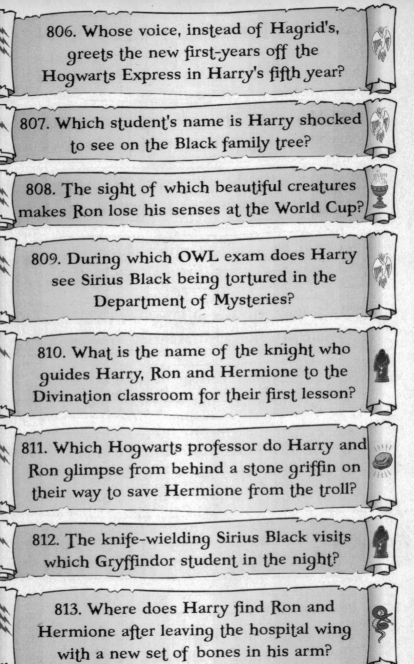

806. Whose voice, instead of Hagrid's, greets the new first-years off the Hogwarts Express in Harry's fifth year?

807. Which student's name is Harry shocked to see on the Black family tree?

808. The sight of which beautiful creatures makes Ron lose his senses at the World Cup?

809. During which OWL exam does Harry see Sirius Black being tortured in the Department of Mysteries?

810. What is the name of the knight who guides Harry, Ron and Hermione to the Divination classroom for their first lesson?

811. Which Hogwarts professor do Harry and Ron glimpse from behind a stone griffin on their way to save Hermione from the troll?

812. The knife-wielding Sirius Black visits which Gryffindor student in the night?

813. Where does Harry find Ron and Hermione after leaving the hospital wing with a new set of bones in his arm?

814. Where does Harry first see Dobby at number four, Privet Drive: in the hedge, on his bed or in the kitchen?

815. What does Draco Malfoy see floating in mid-air outside the Shrieking Shack?

816. Which Hogwarts founder's statue does Harry find in the Chamber of Secrets?

817. What two items does Ron see himself holding in the Mirror of Erised?

818. At Norbert's birth who is peeping through Hagrid's window?

819. Where is Harry when he overhears Professor Snape's account of Sirius Black's capture at Hogwarts?

820. Who does Harry fall out with before the first Triwizard challenge: Ron, Sirius Black or Dumbledore?

821. Seen by Harry in the Pensieve, who claims that Professor Snape is a Death Eater?

822. Name the Death Eater that Hagrid recognises making contact with the giants.

823. Which Ministry official does Harry bump into as he steps off the Knight Bus outside The Leaky Cauldron?

824. Whose hand appears in the flames just after Sirius Black's head vanishes from the Gryffindor fireplace?

825. Which professor does Harry meet on his first visit to The Leaky Cauldron?

826. Which escaped Death Eater is Lord Voldemort seen praising in Harry's dream?

827. Which two Gryffindors react almost as badly as Harry to the appearance of the Dementor on the Hogwarts Express?

828. Does Ron eventually get Viktor Krum's autograph?

829. What does Harry discover scratched into a tap in Moaning Myrtle's bathroom?

830. Which teacher discovers the first-year student, Colin Creevey, petrified on the stairs?

831. Who is Mrs Weasley happy to find signing books in Flourish and Blotts?

832. Which Ravenclaw prefect is hospitalised with Hermione in the second attack of the Basilisk?

833. In which shop in Knockturn Alley does Harry see Draco Malfoy and his father?

834. Hermione brings whom to The Three Broomsticks to see Harry on Valentine's Day?

835. Who enters Harry's carriage of the Hogwarts Express at the very moment that he is splattered with Stinksap?

836. Whom does Harry see Professor Snape talking to in the Forbidden Forest?

837. Whose head appears in the Gryffindor fireplace and talks to Harry shortly before the first Triwizard task?

838. Who does Harry see sneaking towards the dragon enclosure before the first task of the Tournament?

839. Which two Gryffindors does Harry see ogling the Firebolt in Quality Quidditch Supplies?

840. Whom does Harry see trotting beside the black dog by the Forbidden Forest?

841. Which teacher is first to appear on the scene after Ron has knocked out the troll?

842. Who offers Harry, Ron, Hermione and Ginny Weasley his autograph in the Spell Damage ward of St Mungo's?

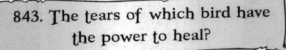

Rescues and Remedies

843. The tears of which bird have the power to heal?

844. Which chess piece does Ron take the place of in the bid to rescue the Philosopher's Stone?

845. Who rescues Harry from the Dursleys in a flying car?

846. What does Hagrid give his dragon Norbert in case he gets lonely?

847. Which Hogwarts' ghost comes to Harry's aid at the bottom of the lake?

848. On the Hogwarts Express, Professor Lupin uses the Patronus Charm against what?

849. Who gives Sirius Black a newspaper in Azkaban?

850. What does Fawkes drop at Harry's feet in the Chamber of Secrets?

851. Who fakes their tears to make Professor Umbridge go into the Forbidden Forest?

852. What is the last item that Harry crams into the Weasleys' flying car before escaping from number four, Privet Drive?

853. What does Harry pull out of the Sorting Hat to fight the Basilisk?

854. What item of clothing does Hermione leave out for Hogwarts' house-elves in the hope of setting them free?

855. How many members of the Order rescue Harry from the Dursleys': three, six or nine?

856. Harry sends a letter to whom when his scar burns during the night at Privet Drive?

857. After fighting Lord Voldemort in the Ministry, what object does Dumbledore use as a Portkey to get Harry back to Hogwarts?

858. Whose life did James Potter save, according to Dumbledore?

859. According to Madam Pomfrey, what is the best remedy after a brush with Dementors?

860. Lucius Malfoy sets Dobby free by throwing which item of Harry's clothing?

861. Who rescues Hermione from the lake during the second task of the Tournament?

862. Who saves Peter Pettigrew's life in the Shrieking Shack: Harry, Professor Snape, Professor Lupin or Dumbledore?

863. What object does Harry summon in the graveyard to escape the Death Eaters?

864. In the Atrium of the Ministry, which statue comes to life to protect Harry: the house-elf, the centaur or the wizard?

865. What does Ron buy from the Magical Menagerie to cure Scabbers?

866. How long does Harry spend at the Burrow after his rescue by flying car: one day, one week or one month?

867. What power protects Harry from the touch of the possessed Professor Quirrell, according to Dumbledore?

868. What is written on the Ministry visitor's badge given to Harry when he comes to rescue his godfather?

869. Which chess piece bashes Ron on the head enabling Harry to go on and rescue the Philosopher's Stone?

870. Who rescues Harry and Hermione from the centaurs in the Forest?

871. What heals Harry's serpent wound in the Chamber of Secrets?

872. Harry and which five members of the DA rescue Sirius Black from the Ministry?

873. Does Dobby give Harry back his friends' letters?

874. On what creature does Harry practise his Patronus Charm with Professor Lupin?

875. Who claims to have helped Professor Sprout give first aid to the Whomping Willow after it's hit by the Ford Anglia?

876. To the dismay of Harry, Ron and Hermione, who embraces Sirius Black in the Shrieking Shack?

877. What magic word does Ron use to disarm the troll in the girls' toilet?

878. Who lent Hagrid the motorbike on which he carries the baby Harry to the safety of number four, Privet Drive?

879. Who does Harry rescue from the bottom of the lake?

880. Viewed in the Penseive: who helps the 15 year old Severus Snape when he is humiliated by Sirius Black and James Potter?

881. What does Professor Lupin give Harry to make him feel better after he sees the Dementor on the Hogwarts Express?

882. Name three members of the Order who come to Harry's rescue in the Dais Room.

883. What item does Professor McGonagall conjure to remove the petrified form of Nearly Headless Nick from the corridor?

884. What colour sparks are the final signal for the Advance Guard to leave the Dursleys' for Grimmauld Place?

885. Which professor races across the Hogwarts lawn to Hagrid's defence only to be hit by four Stunners?

886. Which statue pins Bellatrix Lestrange to the ground in the Atrium of the Ministry: the wizard, the witch or the goblin?

887. What saves Harry and Ron from the eight-legged children of Aragog?

888. How many Galleons reward does the Ministry offer for information leading to the recapture of the escaped Death Eaters?

889. Who's late arrival at the battle against the Death Eaters gives hope to Neville Longbottom and Harry?

Dark Arts and Death

 890. Most witches and wizards refer to Lord Voldemort by what name?

 891. What is the appearance of the spectral black dog said to prophesy?

892. Name the three Death Eaters with sons in Harry's school year.

 893. What was Lord Voldemort's middle name?

894. What is the Dementors' 'last and worst' weapon called?

895. 'There is no good and evil, there is only power.' Who says this to Harry?

896. Was Sirius Black's younger brother, Regulus, a Death Eater?

897. Which Triwizard champion dies in the Tournament?

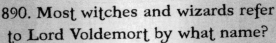 898. What is the name of the mythical black dog said to haunt churchyards?

899. How many Muggles was Sirius Black said to have killed before his arrest by the Magical Law Enforcement Patrol?

900. Name the first ingredient added to the cauldron in the graveyard that returns Lord Voldemort to his body.

901. In which pub does Hagrid tell the hooded stranger about Fluffy?

902. The first victim of the Basilisk was petrified. Who was it?

903. What does Harry glimpse in the stands before Dementors invade the Quidditch pitch?

904. Which of Lord Voldemort's parents was a Muggle: his father or his mother?

905. What is the name that appears on the first page of the book that Harry and Ron find in Moaning Myrtle's toilet?

906. In which village is the Riddle House?

907. What was the name of the Riddles' gardener?

908. Who is the second victim of the Basilisk?

909. While the Death Eaters are running amok at the World Cup, which student do Harry, Ron and Hermione find in the woods?

910. With whom does Lord Voldemort share his original name?

911. What form does the Dark Mark take?

912. Who discovered the Riddles' dead bodies: the gardener, the maid or the cook?

913. Who kills Barty Crouch (Snr)?

914. Nearly Headless Nick was struck on the neck by an axe 24, 54 or 45 times?

915. What is the name of Buckbeak's executioner?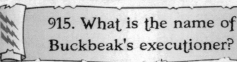

916. Who opened the Chamber of Secrets the second time?

917. What is the name of the severed hand that gives light only to the beholder?

918. What was the name of the Riddles' village pub?

919. Who kills Frank Bryce?

920. What newsworthy event happens on the day of Harry's first visit to Diagon Alley?

921. What was the first name of Lord Voldemort's grandfather?

922. Name the backpacking Ministry witch killed by Lord Voldemort.

923. Which members of his family did Lord Voldemort kill in the Riddle House?

924. Death Eaters parade which Muggle family in mid-air at the World Cup?

925. Barty Crouch (Jnr) and three others used the Cruciatus curse on which married couple?

926. How many Death Eaters does the *Daily Prophet* report escaping from Azkaban?

927. By what name does Dobby refer to Lord Voldemort?

928. Which member of the Order is meant to be watching Harry when Dementors invade Little Whinging?

929. On which street would you find the shop Borgin and Burkes?

930. What is the name of the Auror who put Igor Karkaroff in Azkaban?

931. Who orders the Dementors to go after Harry at Privet Drive?

932. How many years ago was the Chamber of Secrets last opened: 50, 100 or 150?

933. Whose wand is used to conjure the Dark Mark at the World Cup?

934. With what item does Harry destroy Tom Riddle in the Chamber of Secrets?

935. What anagram of TOM MARVOLO RIDDLE gives Harry the identity of his enemy in the Chamber of Secrets?

936. Which member of the Order ends up in St Mungo's after the battle in the Department of Mysteries?

937. According to the writing on a corridor wall on Hogwarts second floor, whose enemies must beware?

938. Who planted Tom Riddle's diary in Ginny Weasley's old Transfiguration book?

939. Name the prime suspect found at the scene where the Dark Mark was conjured.

940. Who is Lord Voldemort's 'most faithful servant'?

941. What is the name of the former Death Eater turned Durmstrang Headmaster?

942. Who kills Sirius Black?

943. Whose screams were responsible for Hogsmeade villagers thinking that the Shrieking Shack was haunted?

944. What plant strangles Ministry worker Broderick Bode in St Mungo's?

945. Which Hogwarts student is possessed by Lord Voldemort?

Who's Who?

946. Whose nickname was Prongs?

947. Beginning with 'O', what is Madame Maxime's first name?

948. What is Goyle's first name?

949. Beginning with 'N', what is the first name of Draco Malfoy's mother?

950. Beginning with 'F', what is the first name of Hagrid's mother?

951. By what name does the witch Nymphadora prefer to be called?

952. Who was Sirius Black's best friend at Hogwarts?

953. Who is heir of Slytherin?

954. Who did Olive Hornby tease?

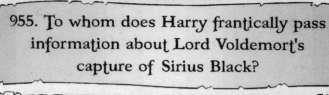

955. To whom does Harry frantically pass information about Lord Voldemort's capture of Sirius Black?

956. How old was Sirius Black when he tried to kill Severus Snape?

957. Who shoved Neville Longbottom off Blackpool pier as a young boy?

958. Who interrupts Harry's conversation with the head of Sirius Black in Gryffindor common room?

959. Who interrupts Ginny Weasley at breakfast when she is trying to tell Harry about the Chamber of Secrets?

960. Who ransacks Harry's possessions in the Gryffindor dormitory?

961. What is Crabbe's first name?

962. Which girl becomes a Slytherin prefect along with Draco Malfoy?

963. Perenelle is the aged wife of which great wizard?

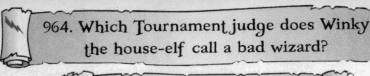

964. Which Tournament judge does Winky the house-elf call a bad wizard?

965. Who is Trevor?

966. Beginning with 'P', what is Madam Pomfrey's first name?

967. Who is the driver of the Knight Bus: Ernie Prang or Stan Shunpike?

968. Was Cassandra Trelawney Professor Trelawney's mother, grandmother or great-great-grandmother?

969. Who does Mr Weasley attack in Flourish and Blotts?

970. Who tells the Minister for Magic that Sirius Black bewitched Harry, Ron and Hermione with a Confundus Charm?

971. Who slashed the portrait of the Fat Lady?

972. On the first night of the fifth year, which room-mate argues with Harry over allegations made in the *Daily Prophet*?

973. Name two of the teachers patrolling the outside of the Triwizard maze.

974. Who owes Fred and George Weasley money for a bet at the World Cup final?

975. To which other wizarding school did Mr Malfoy consider sending his son Draco?

976. With whom does Hagrid trek to the land of the giants?

977. Whose sword does Harry pull out of the Sorting Hat in the Chamber of Secrets?

978. Who wakes Harry on the morning of the second challenge?

979. To which teacher does Harry take the injured Hedwig?

980. Which Triwizard judge offers Harry pointers before the first challenge?

981. Who is a governor of Hogwarts: Lucius Malfoy or Arthur Weasley?

982. Which two teachers take the weeping Professor Trelawney back to her room after her dismissal from Hogwarts?

983. What is the name of Aragog's wife?

984. Whose nickname was Padfoot?

985. Who sent Mrs Dursley the Howler after the Dementors visited Little Whinging?

986. Which two Gryffindors are not impressed by Harry and Ron's crash landing into the Whomping Willow?

987. Who wears a tea cosy on his head?

988. Which Creevey brother falls into the lake before the Sorting Ceremony?

989. Which Hufflepuff student accuses Harry of being the heir of Slytherin?

990. Who threatens to dog Harry's footsteps in his fifth year?

991. Which Hufflepuff boy quizzes Harry about Lord Voldemort in the Hog's Head?

992. Who appears under Professor Quirrell's turban?

993. Name the three champions that Harry competes with in the Tournament.

994. Whose nickname was Wormtail?

995. Who throws Tom Riddle's diary down Moaning Myrtle's toilet?

996. Who comes to Hogwarts with Mrs Weasley to wish Harry good luck before the third Triwizard task?

997. What is the name of the journalist who writes the report about Ministry blunders at the World Cup?

998. Which member of the Durmstrang delegation has Ron seen before?

999. Who is the only known maker of the Philosopher's Stone?

1000. Who built the Chamber of Secrets?

1001. Who was Lily and James Potter's treacherous Secret-Keeper?

Answers

Harry, Ron and Hermione

1. Green
2. September
3. Hermione and Ron
4. Viktor Krum
5. Holly
6. Six
7. An otter
8. Avada Kedavra
9. The Chudley Cannons
10. Lily and James Potter
11. A Nimbus Two Thousand
12. A Shooting Star
13. A lightning bolt
14. Granger
15. Halloween
16. Five
17. A stag
18. 112%
19. Harry
20. Ginger
21. Maroon
22. Goyle
23. A boa constrictor
24. His mother
25. Arthur and Molly Weasley
26. Hagrid
27. Bill Weasley
28. Evans
29. Charlie Weasley
30. Her second
31. Two
32. Sirius Black
33. Ginny Weasley
34. Pidwigeon or Pig
35. France
36. Butterbeer
37. A unicorn
38. The Burrow
39. One
40. Professor McGonagall
41. His arm
42. July 31st
43. Slytherin
44. His mother's
45. Hermione
46. Ottery St Catchpole
47. Godric's Hollow
48. Percy Weasley
49. Stonewall High
50. His father
51. His right arm
52. Professor Trelawney
53. Neville Longbottom
54. A teaspoon
55. Wheezy
56. Hagrid
57. His 12th birthday
58. Dudley's birthday
59. Grimmauld Place
60. Red
61. Gryffindor
62. A phoenix

Hogwarts, Houses and Professors

63. Gryffindor, Hufflepuff, Ravenclaw and Slytherin
64. A lion, an eagle, a badger and a snake
65. September 1st
66. Five
67. 'Hogwarts, Hogwarts, Hoggy Warty Hogwarts'
68. Winged boars
69. 142
70. Dumbledore
71. A badger
72. Hagrid

73. Gryffindor (bold), Ravenclaw (fair), Hufflepuff (sweet), Slytherin (shrewd)
74. Madam Hooch
75. A cat
76. Care of Magical Creatures
77. Round
78. Divination
79. Professor Lupin
80. Professor Moody
81. Professor Sprout
82. Rubeus
83. Hogsmeade
84. The dungeon
85. Professor Quirrell's
86. Professor Moody
87. Professor McGonagall
88. Professor Binns
89. Firenze, the centaur
90. Dumbledore's office
91. A turban
92. Professor Snape
93. 12
94. Professor Snape
95. Professor Kettleburn
96. The Whomping Willow
97. Pince
98. Professor McGonagall's
99. 39 years
100. West
101. Gryffindor
102. A stone gargoyle
103. Armando Dippet
104. Bewildered
105. Defence Against the Dark Arts
106. The Room of Requirement
107. Mad-Eye Moody
108. 'Out of Order'
109. Pomfrey
110. Argus
111. Dumbledore
112. Sir Cadogan
113. The Entrance Hall
114. Gryffindor
115. Professor McGonagall
116. Gryffindor
117. Blue
118. Argus Filch
119. Defence Against the Dark Arts
120. 6
121. Professor McGonagall
122. Professor Lupin
123. The seventh
124. Hannah Abbot
125. Grawp
126. Circular
127. Professor Grubbly-Plank
128. Five
129. Brother
130. Remedial Potions
131. A witch
132. 100
133. Grindelwald
134. The Triwizard Tournament
135. The four founders of Hogwarts
136. Tenpin bowling
137. Slytherin
138. Peeves
139. Professor Trelawney

The Dursleys
140. Four
141. His tenth birthday
142. Bulldogs
143. The *Daily Mail*
144. His PlayStation
145. Little Whinging
146. Mrs Dursley
147. Grunnings
148. Straw hat or knobbly stick
149. A television set
150. Drills
151. Ripper
152. The Masons
153. Smeltings
154. Figg

155. Ron
156. Map-read
157. The Railview Hotel
158. A Dementor
159. Boxing
160. An electric fire
161. Criminal Boys
162. 39
163. Mrs Figg
164. 5
165. Surrey
166. A wine glass
167. Petunia
168. Piers Polkiss
169. Mr Dursley
170. Dudley
171. She has a broken leg
172. The Weasleys'

Magical Places and Transport

173. Flourish and Blotts
174. Gringotts
175. The Knight Bus
176. Platform nine and three quarters
177. 11a.m.
178. Ollivanders
179. A joke shop
180. The Order of the Phoenix
181. Hogsmeade
182. Paddington station
183. St Mungo's
184. Azkaban
185. Floo powder, Broomstick, Apparition and Portkey
186. The Three Broomsticks
187. Floo powder
188. St Mungo's
189. Healers
190. Wiltshire
191. A sweetshop
192. Purple
193. Zonko's
194. Gringotts
195. Wizarding Wireless Network
196. Beauxbatons and Durmstrang
197. Hogsmeade station
198. The Hog's Head
199. The Shrieking Shack
200. Broomstick
201. Stoatshead Hill
202. The Philosopher's Stone
203. Weasleys' Wizarding Wheezes
204. Floo powder
205. The Leaky Cauldron
206. By ship
207. Kreacher
208. Egypt
209. Dumbledore's office and Grimmauld Place
210. Purge & Dowse Ltd
211. Portkeys
212. Madam Puddifoot's
213. Hogsmeade
214. Devon
215. Yes
216. Dobby
217. Griphook
218. Mrs Black
219. Stagecoach
220. By Muggle taxi
221. By underground train
222. Tom
223. North
224. Greed
225. Flying carpets
226. Two
227. 1
228. The Leaky Cauldron
229. Ice cream
230. Scarlet
231. The Black family
232. By flying car
233. Buckbeak
234. The Malfoys
235. Thestrals
236. Uncomfortably hot

Magical Items and Equipment

237. Wood
238. A large marble
239. A Pocket Sneakoscope
240. A Pensieve
241. A pink umbrella
242. A Ton-Tongue Toffee
243. An empty sweet-wrapper
244. A Foe-Glass
245. Sirius Black
246. A Silver Arrow
247. Seven
248. Fawkes
249. Hermione
250. A flute
251. Fainting Fancies
252. The Marauder's Map and the Invisibility Cloak
253. A Veela
254. A Filibuster firework
255. 17
256. A dragon
257. A Put-Outer
258. Mr Weasley's Ford Anglia car
259. Every Flavour
260. A fang earring
261. Gold
262. An old boot
263. 29
264. Leprechaun gold
265. Quick-Quotes Quill
266. Three
267. Willow
268. Flesh-Eatin' Slug Repellent
269. Spellotape
270. 16 inches
271. Yew
272. 7 Galleons
273. The *Quibbler*
274. An old rubber tyre
275. *Mimnilus mimbletonia*
276. Omnioculars
277. I show not your face but your heart's desire
278. A camera
279. The Firebolt
280. Three
281. A two-way mirror
282. 14 inches
283. A Time-Turner
284. A Revealer
285. Blood-red
286. 'Mortal Peril'
287. The Philosopher's Stone

Quidditch

288. Beater
289. Seven
290. Scarlet
291. Black
292. Chasers
293. Canary yellow
294. Oliver Wood
295. Nimbus Two Thousand and One
296. Three
297. A Quaffle
298. Cleansweep Five
299. November
300. 150
301. The Firebolt
302. 700
303. Orange
304. Beaters
305. Cedric Diggory
306. The Bludger (enchanted by Dobby)
307. Cho Chang
308. Dumbledore
309. 30 years
310. Four
311. Seeker
312. Transylvania
313. Ireland
314. Dumbledore
315. Gryffindor and Hufflepuff
316. Lee Jordan
317. Harry, Katie Bell, Angelina Johnson, Alicia Spinnet, Fred Weasley, George Weasley and Oliver Wood

318. Angelina Johnson
319. Ludo Bagman
320. Red
321. The Wimbourne Wasps
322. Seven
323. Ginny Weasley
324. Ireland
325. 'Potter for President'
326. Cho Chang
327. The Wronski Feint
328. Viktor Krum
329. Chaser
330. Slytherin and Gryffindor
331. 100,000
332. Angelina Johnson
333. 'Weasley is our King'
334. Four
335. Puddlemere United
336. 14
337. Ravenclaw
338. St Mungo's
339. Seamus Finnigan
340. 50 feet
341. Ron
342. The Malfoys
343. Viktor Krum
344. Beater
345. Cobbing

Triwizards

346. The Goblet of Fire
347. Five
348. Halloween
349. 1,000 Galleons
350. Three
351. October
352. Blood-red
353. Golden wands
354. Slytherin
355. In a golden egg
356. Dumbledore, Karkaroff, Maxime, Bagman and Crouch
357. Madame Maxime
358. 'POTTER STINKS'
359. Professor Karkaroff
360. The second
361. Ludo Bagman and Barty Crouch (Snr)
362. Viktor Krum
363. Harry
364. June
365. Mr Ollivander

Charms and Curses

366. The full Body-Bind
367. The Imperius curse
368. 'Expelliarmus!'
369. 'Accio!'
370. Professors Sprout, Flitwick and Quirrell
371. The Conjunctivitus curse
372. Clean
373. Viktor Krum
374. The Flame-Freezing Charm
375. 'Impervius!'
376. 'Incendio!'
377. 'Expecto Patronum'
378. The Cruciatus curse
379. A Tickling Charm
380. Professor Snape
381. 'Lumos!"
382. 'Riddikulus!'
383. A Memory Charm
384. The Cruciatus curse
385. 'Wingardium Leviosa!'
386. An Engorgement Charm
387. 'Obliviate!'
388. Seals
389. 'Enervate'
390. A Confundus Charm
391. The Imperius curse
392. The Fidelius Charm

393. Avada Kedavra
394. 'Petrificus Totalus!'
395. 'Prior Incantato!'
396. A Shield Charm
397. The Impediment Jinx
398. The Summoning Charm
399. 'Rictusempra!'
400. Red and green
401. Professor Lockhart
402. Neville Longbottom
403. Mammals
404. Professor Flitwick
405. The Imperius curse, the Cruciatus curse and Avada Kedavra (the killing curse)
406. The Bubble-Head Charm
407. The Dark Mark
408. The Cheering Charm
409. Stunning Spells
410. 'Protego!'
411. The Disillusionment Charm
412. A Hover Charm
413. The Patronus Charm
414. Pain
415. The Impediment Jinx
416. Avada Kedavra
417. 'SNEAK'
418. Professor Snape

Transformations and Potions

419. Polyjuice Potion
420. Skiving Snackboxes
421. A cat
422. Millicent Bulstrode
423. A rat
424. A Confusing Concoction
425. Long white beards
426. Three
427. Salamander blood
428. A pig
429. Wolfsbane Potion
430. Gillyweed
431. Animagi
432. A Metamorph-magus
433. Chocolate cake
434. Sleeping
435. A goat
436. A mouse
437. The Mandrake or Mandragora
438. Professor Snape

439. Bubotuber
440. 7
441. Polyjuice Potion
442. Professor Snape
443. A beetle
444. 2
445. Veritaserum
446. 1 hour
447. A pop
448. One
449. Neville Longbottom
450. An Egyptian mummy
451. Skele-Gro
452. The full moon
453. A ferret
454. A month
455. A vegetable
456. Pepperup Potion
457. Professor McGonagall

The Ministry of Magic

458. Cornelius Fudge
459. Ludo Bagman
460. A red telephone box
461. By paper aeroplane
462. Policemen
463. Brains
464. The Muggle Protection Act
465. Barty Crouch (Snr)

466. A regurgitating public toilet
467. Lucius Malfoy
468. W
469. A bowler hat
470. Albania
471. Unspeakables
472. Fireplaces
473. Level Ten
474. 62442
475. Tom
476. The Department of Mysteries
477. Barty Crouch (Snr)
478. Weatherby
479. Muggle Artefacts Office
480. Improper Use of Magic Office
481. Arthur Weasley
482. Barty Crouch (Snr)
483. Lucius Malfoy
484. Delores Umbridge
485. Sturgis Podmore
486. Convict
487. Ludo Bagman
488. Millicent Bagnold
489. Harry and Viktor Krum
490. The Court Scribe
491. Bellatrix Lestrange
492. Co-operation

493. Lucius Malfoy
494. Perkins
495. 97
496. Eric Munch
497. Cornelius Fudge
498. Kingsley Shacklebolt
499. Cornelius Fudge
500. The Atrium
501. 10,000 Galleons
502. The Accidental Magic Reversal Department

Creatures and Ghosts
503. Gryffindor
504. A dragon
505. Salamanders
506. A crack
507. Bats
508. A dragon
509. The staff room
510. Single-malt whisky
511. Dragon
512. Leprechauns
513. A boarhound
514. The Bloody Baron
515. Fawkes
516. Romania
517. A Boggart
518. A giant squid
519. House-elves
520. A Basilisk
521. Nagini
522. Nifflers

523. 12
524. A Hinkypunk
525. Silver
526. A spider
527. Eagle
528. A Grindylow
529. A Swedish Short-Snout
530. Thestrals
531. Bane
532. Winky
533. Moaning Myrtle
534. 500
535. Fluffy
536. Fang
537. 80
538. The Weasleys' owl
539. A spider
540. Firenze
541. Local deliveries
542. Female
543. Doxys
544. The Bloody Baron
545. A Boggart
546. You die
547. Chicken blood
548. Errol
549. Gobbledegook
550. A chicken
551. A rabbit
552. Gold
553. Welsh Green
554. A Knarl
555. A serpent

556. Sir Nicholas de Mimsy-Porpington
557. Blood
558. A troll
559. Cornish pixies
560. Wherever there has been bloodshed
561. Gold
562. Bowtruckles
563. Welsh Green or Hebridean Black
564. *A History of Magic*
565. The Basilisk
566. A house-elf
567. Hermes
568. Hufflepuff
569. A Hippogriff
570. A Blast-Ended Skrewt
571. Silver
572. Buckbeak
573. The crowing of a rooster

Lessons and Rules
574. Magic
575. Acceptable
576. Flying
577. Society for the Promotion of Elfish Welfare
578. An owl, a cat or a toad
579. 17 years old
580. Greenhouses

581. North Tower
582. His wrist
583. No
584. Dreadful
585. Herbology
586. 6p.m.
587. Draco Malfoy
588. Five (they gain ten and lose five)
589. The Forbidden Forest
590. Divination
591. Alchemy
592. Occlumency
593. Hufflepuff
594. The Order of Merlin
595. 17 years old
596. Nastily Exhausting Wizarding Test
597. Care of Magical Creatures and Divination
598. Harry, Fred Weasley and George Weasley
599. Legilimency
600. The future
601. Herbology
602. A Patronus
603. Becoming an Auror
604. Divination
605. Two
606. Professors Lockhart and Snape

607. Transfiguration
608. 9p.m.
609. High Inquisitor
610. An Age Line
611. Astronomy
612. *Magical Me*
613. Ordinary Wizarding Level
614. Exceeds Expectations
615. A Squib
616. The Inquisitorial Squad
617. Parvati Patil and Lavender Brown
618. *One Thousand Magical Herbs and Fungi*
619. Examinations
620. 3 feet
621. 12
622. Two
623. Five
624. Treasurer
625. *The Dark Forces: A Guide to Self-Protection*
626. An Order of Suspension
627. The History of Magic classroom
628. NEWT
629. Nearly Headless Nick
630. An egg cup

Festivities, Feasts and Fun

631. 12
632. Cats
633. Vomit
634. The Weird Sisters
635. Chocolate cake
636. Halloween
637. A hand-knitted sweater
638. Milkman
639. Ginny Weasley and Colin Creevey
640. Penelope Clearwater
641. Harry
642. Ron, Neville, Dean and Seamus
643. A newspaper cutting
644. Fred and George Weasley
645. 46
646. Hagrid
647. Padma Patil
648. Neville Longbottom and Hermione
649. Professor Snape
650. Hot chocolate
651. Plugs
652. 'Mischief managed'
653. Sherbet Lemons
654. Parvati Patil
655. The Room of Requirement

656. Hermione
657. Angelina Johnson
658. A homework planner
659. Fred and George Weasley
660. His father
661. A Quidditch move
662. Ireland
663. Plumbers
664. Four
665. Socks
666. Romania
667. Periwinkle-blue
668. A patchwork quilt
669. A toothpick
670. Ginny Weasley
671. Head Hockey
672. Tables
673. Professor Trelawney
674. Rita Skeeter
675. Fleur Delacour
676. Dean Thomas
677. Colin Creevey
678. Dean Thomas
679. Dumbledore
680. Lee Jordan
681. Fred Weasley
682. Sirius Black
683. 5
684. Dobby
685. A Cleansweep Eleven
686. Percy Weasley
687. Cho Chang

688. 700
689. Cho Chang
690. Peeves
691. Dobby
692. Ogdens Old Firewhisky
693. Sweden
694. Ginny Weasley
695. Fire
696. Egypt

Secrets and Danger

697. A troll
698. Under a loose floorboard under his bed
699. Giants
700. A snake
701. The Restricted Section
702. Gryffindor
703. Snuffles
704. Professor Lockhart
705. Ginny Weasley
706. Dumbledore
707. The trophy room
708. Neville Longbottom
709. Professor Snape
710. The reptile house at the zoo
711. The Quibbler
712. Neville Longbottom
713. Honeydukes
714. The dragons

715. A killing
716. The prefects' bathroom
717. Argus Filch's
718. Seven
719. Snivellus
720. Dumbledore's Army
721. A year
722. Argus Filch and Professor Snape
723. Harry's father, James Potter
724. Neville Longbottom's
725. Moony
726. The chief giant
727. Professor Trelawney
728. Sirius Black
729. Dobby
730. Sirius Black
731. Three
732. Professor Lockhart's office
733. Dumbledore
734. Hermione
735. Crookshanks
736. Professor Snape
737. Animagi
738. Parseltongue
739. Percy Weasley
740. A pear
741. Professor Snape
742. 'Pure-blood'
743. 'Mudblood'
744. June 13th

745. Barty Crouch (Jnr)
746. 711
747. Tonks and Remus Lupin
748. The veil
749. Dumbledore's Army
750. The Infirmary
751. Professor Lupin
752. The Shrieking Shack
753. His trunk
754. Whispers
755. Hidden under dirty bandages

Caught and Punished

756. Magic
757. Ron's
758. 12
759. The Patronus Charm
760. Scabbers
761. His blood
762. Professor McGonagall
763. Professor Karkaroff
764. Professor Umbridge
765. De-gnome the garden
766. He gives her clothes (setting her free)
767. Ten

768. The Department of Mysteries
769. The *Evening Prophet*
770. Harry and Hermione
771. An Auror
772. Azkaban
773. August
774. Percy Weasley
775. The Dementor's Kiss
776. Mr Weasley
777. 20
778. The cupboard under the stairs
779. Marietta Edgecombe
780. Professor Snape
781. Willy Widdershins
782. Dumbledore
783. Underage Wizardry
784. Professor Flitwick
785. Ron
786. George
787. The hospital wing
788. Contacted Hogwarts by owl
789. Professor Lupin and Ron
790. Kingsley Shacklebolt
791. Scabbers

792. The eyes
793. Dumbledore and Professor Moody
794. 1a.m.
795. Dumbledore
796. A Howler
797. A week

Encounters and Sightings

798. A unicorn
799. The Grim
800. Madam Malkin's Robes for All Occasions
801. Himself
802. Amos Diggory's
803. Lachlan the Lanky
804. Magnolia Crescent
805. Professor Lupin
806. Professor Grubbly-Plank's
807. Draco Malfoy
808. Veela
809. History of Magic
810. Sir Cadogan
811. Professor Snape
812. Ron
813. Moaning Myrtle's toilet
814. In the hedge
815. Harry's head
816. Salazar Slytherin

817. The House Cup and the Quidditch Cup
818. Draco Malfoy
819. The hospital wing
820. Ron
821. Professor Karkaroff
822. Macnair
823. Cornelius Fudge
824. Professor Umbridge's
825. Professor Quirrell
826. Rookwood
827. Ginny Weasley and Neville Longbottom
828. Yes
829. A snake
830. Professor McGonagall
831. Gilderoy Lockhart
832. Penelope Clearwater
833. Borgin and Burkes
834. Luna Lovegood and Rita Skeeter
835. Cho Chang
836. Professor Quirrell
837. Sirius Black's
838. Professor Karkaroff

839. Seamus Finnigan and Dean Thomas
840. Crookshanks
841. Professor McGonagall
842. Professor Lockhart

Rescues and Remedies

843. The phoenix
844. The black knight
845. Ron, Fred and George Weasley
846. A teddy bear
847. Moaning Myrtle
848. A Dementor
849. Cornelius Fudge
850. The Sorting Hat
851. Hermione
852. Hedwig's cage
853. The Gryffindor sword
854. Knitted hats
855. Nine
856. Sirius Black
857. The golden wizard's head
858. Professor Snape's
859. Chocolate
860. His sock
861. Viktor Krum
862. Harry
863. The Triwizard Cup
864. The wizard

865. Rat Tonic
866. One month
867. Love
868. 'Harry Potter, Rescue Mission'
869. The white queen
870. Grawp
871. Phoenix tears
872. Ron, Hermione, Ginny Weasley, Luna Lovegood and Neville Longbottom
873. No
874. A Boggart
875. Professor Lockhart
876. Professor Lupin
877. 'Wingardium Leviosa!'
878. Sirius Black
879. Ron and Gabrielle Delacour
880. Lily Evans
881. Chocolate
882. Sirius Black, Professor Lupin, Professor Moody, Tonks, Kingsley Shacklebolt, and Dumbledore
883. A large fan
884. Green
885. Professor McGonagall
886. The witch

887. Mr Weasley's Ford Anglia
888. 1,000 Galleons
889. Dumbledore's

Dark Arts and Death

890. You-Know-Who
891. Death
892. Malfoy, Goyle and Crabbe
893. Marvolo
894. The Dementor's Kiss
895. Professor Quirrell
896. Yes
897. Cedric Diggory
898. The Grim
899. 12
900. Crushed bone of Tom Riddle, Lord Voldemort's father
901. The Hog's Head
902. Mrs Norris
903. A black dog
904. Father
905. T.M. Riddle
906. Little Hangleton
907. Frank Bryce
908. Colin Creevey
909. Draco Malfoy
910. His father
911. A skull
912. The maid
913. Barty Crouch (Jnr)
914. 45
915. Macnair

916. Ginny Weasley
917. The Hand of Glory
918. The Hanged Man
919. Lord Voldemort
920. The Gringotts break-in
921. Marvolo
922. Bertha Jorkins
923. His father, grandmother and grandfather
924. The Roberts
925. The Long-bottoms
926. Ten
927. He Who Must Not Be Named
928. Mundungus Fletcher
929. Knockturn Alley
930. Alastair Moody
931. Professor Umbridge
932. 50
933. Harry's
934. The Basilisk fang
935. I AM LORD VOLDEMORT
936. Tonks
937. The enemies of the heir
938. Lucius Malfoy
939. Winky
940. Barty Crouch (Jnr)

941. Professor Karkaroff
942. Bellatrix Lestrange
943. Remus Lupin's
944. Devil's Snare
945. Ginny Weasley

Who's Who?

946. Harry's father, James Potter
947. Olympe
948. Gregory
949. Narcissa
950. Fridwulfa
951. Tonks
952. Harry's father, James Potter
953. Lord Voldemort
954. Moaning Myrtle
955. Professor Snape
956. 16
957. His Great Uncle Algie
958. Ron
959. Percy Weasley
960. Ginny Weasley
961. Vincent
962. Pansy Parkinson
963. Nicolas Flamel
964. Ludo Bagman
965. Neville Longbottom's toad
966. Poppy
967. Ernie Prang

968. Great-great-grandmother
969. Lucius Malfoy
970. Professor Snape
971. Sirius Black
972. Seamus Finnigan
973. Professor Moody, Professor McGonagall, Professor Flitwick and Hagrid
974. Ludo Bagman
975. Durmstrang
976. Madame Maxime
977. Godric Gryffindor's
978. Dobby
979. Professor Grubbly-Plank
980. Ludo Bagman
981. Lucius Malfoy
982. Professors McGonagall and Sprout
983. Mosag
984. Sirius Black
985. Dumbledore
986. Percy Weasley and Hermione
987. Dobby
988. Dennis Creevey
989. Ernie Macmillan
990. Draco Malfoy
991. Zacharias Smith
992. Lord Voldemort

993. Viktor Krum, Fleur Delacour and Cedric Diggory
994. Peter Pettigrew's
995. Ginny Weasley
996. Bill Weasley
997. Rita Skeeter
998. Viktor Krum
999. Nicolas Flamel
1000. Salazar Slytherin
1001. Peter Pettigrew

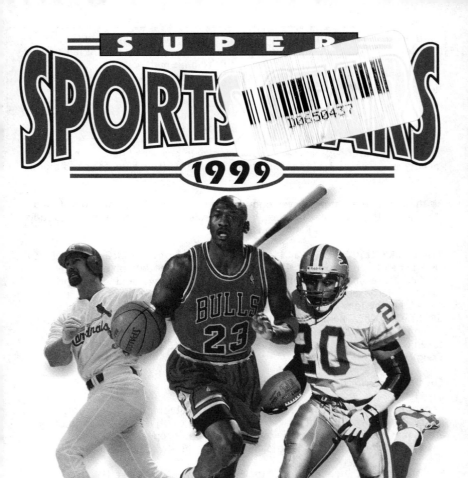

SUPER SPORTS STARS
1999

RICHARD J. BRENNER

AN EAST END PUBLISHING BOOK
SYOSSET, NY

Author's Note: All of the players in this book are gifted athletes, but they all had to work hard, and overcome obstacles to achieve their success. Even Michael Jordan had to bounce back from being cut from his high school basketball team.

You can become a superstar, too, if you want to work for it. And there are lots of areas for you to consider besides athletics. You can help clean up the environment or work for world peace. You can become a musician, a teacher, a doctor, a human rights activist, or a writer. We need superstar ecologists and caregivers much more than we need superstar athletes.

To all people everywhere: May you always play in peace and happiness, walk in beauty, and work to build communities that are free from hate, fear, and bigotry of every type.

With great appreciation to everybody whose time and talents have contributed so much to this book, most especially Eric Macaluso. Thanks are also due to Judy Newman, Liz Loftus, and Randy Lawrence.

PHOTO CREDITS: The cover and interior photograph of Mark McGwire was taken by **Stephen Dunn/ALLSPORT**. The cover and interior photograph of Michael Jordan was taken by **Jonathan Daniel/ALLSPORT**. The cover and interior photograph of Barry Sanders, and the photographs of Sammy Sosa and Derek Jeter were taken by **Tony Inzerillo**. The remaining photographs were supplied by **SPORTSCHROME**: The photographs of Ken Griffey, Jr., and Shaquille O'Neal were taken by **Michael Zito**; the photographs of Brett Favre and Terrell Davis were taken by **Vincent Manniello**; and the photograph of Eric Lindros was taken by **Craig Melvin**.

Cover and interior design by **Eric Macaluso**.

Published by East End Publishing, Ltd., 54 Alexander Dr., Syosset, NY 11791

Printed in the United States of America
ISBN 0-943403-51-0

Mr. Brenner, America's best-selling sportswriter, is the author of more than 50 sports books, including: FOOTBALL SUPERSTARS ALBUM 1998; BASEBALL SUPER-STARS ALBUM 1999; BASKETBALL SUPERSTARS ALBUM 1999; and a series of easy-to-read photo-biographies of: MICHAEL JORDAN; KOBE BRYANT; GRANT HILL; MARK McGWIRE; and SAMMY SOSA.
(All of the above titles are in full color.)

**For a complete order form send $1.00 or a self-addressed stamped envelope to:
East End Publishing, Ltd., 54 Alexander Dr., Syosset, NY 11791.**

SUPER SPORTS STARS
1999

MARK McGWIRE

Mark McGwire has been breaking home run records since he set the Claremont (California) Little League career mark when he was ten years old. Although he concentrated on pitching in high school and his freshman year at the University of Southern California, Mark started swinging the club in his second year with the Trojans and racked up a school-record 19 big flies. The following year Mac annihilated his own record by rapping 32 home runs, raising the bar to a height that still hasn't been matched by any other USC player. "Mark was made for success, and you could see it early on," said Arizona Diamondbacks pitching ace Randy Johnson, a college teammate of Mac's. "It was obvious that he was a major talent."

Three years later, after serving his minor-league apprenticeship, Mac rocketed to success with the Oakland Athletics by blasting a major-league rookie-record 49 home runs, 11 more than any rookie had ever hit in the big leagues. Mark had the chance to join a very exclusive club by going for number 50 on the final day of the 1987 season, but

MARK McGWIRE

ST. LOUIS CARDINALS - FIRST BASEMAN

5

he passed on the opportunity in order to be present at the birth of his son, Matthew. "I'll never have another first child," said Mark, explaining a decision he's never regretted. "But I will have another chance to hit 50 home runs."

Mac had made hitting home runs look so easy during his Rookie-of-the-Year season that reporters began comparing him with the legendary Babe Ruth, who had swatted 60 homers in 1927, and Roger Maris, who, in a singular season of excellence, had eclipsed Ruth's mark by hitting 61 in 1961. But Mac didn't even come close to repeating that level of success over the following eight seasons. While he did have a few good years, he also went through a lot of down times on and off the field, including a divorce, a .201 batting average in 1991, and a series of injuries that cost him the better part of two seasons. At times Mark became so depressed and frustrated that he thought about quitting. "I was in a deep hole," said Mac. "And I didn't know if I could climb out."

With the help of counseling and his own inner reservoir of resolve, however, Mark did find the strength to carve out the footholds he needed to raise his life and his game back onto level ground. He showed just how high he had risen on the field by going yard 52 times in 1996, becoming only the twelfth player in big-league history to reach the half-century mark. Mac ratcheted his game to a higher level the following year by rapping 58 homers, including 24 for the St. Louis Cardinals, who had obtained him in a midseason trade with the A's.

Mac had joined Babe Ruth as the only other player to swat 50 homers in consecutive seasons, and the big question on the minds of baseball fans seemed to be whether he would make a run at 62 in 1998. Although Mac maintained that it was foolish to talk about a record before the season had even begun, he fueled the discussions with an early-season home run binge that sent "Mac mania" sweeping across the country. Wherever the Cardinals played, thousands of fans began showing up hours before games just to watch him blast batting practice pitches to far away places. At the All-Star break, the traditional midpoint of the season, Mac had already scorched 37 home runs, most of them hit so far and high they looked like NASA launchings. "I never saw anybody in all my years of watching baseball that absolutely crushed the ball as much as he does," said Hall of Famer Ted Williams, the last player to hit .400. "I think people go to the ballpark to see if he's going to hit one over the moon."

After Mark had upped his total to 51 on August 20, he took a few moments to cherish his singular accomplishment. "I never dreamed this when I was a kid," said Mac, who had become the only player to hit 50 home runs in three successive years. "I never dreamed this when I was a college or minor-league player. I thought about it going into this season, and I'm so proud that I was able to reach it." And for the first time, even he conceded that Maris's record was finally in reach. "But it's going to be tough," he predicted before roaring on to 60, just in time for a two-game series against Sammy Sosa and the Chicago Cubs.

Over the second half of the season, Mark had been joined in the home run derby by Sosa, who became Mac's friendly rival as well as his smiling supporter. So it was with a poetic sense of timing that Mark lined his record-tying sixty-first and record-breaking sixty-second homers against the Cubs, allowing Sosa to become part of the joyous celebration that rocked Busch Stadium. After a delirious spin around the bases witnessed by millions of excited television viewers, Mark scooped up his son, Matthew, the Cardinals' acting batboy, waved to his parents, and then went into the stands to embrace the grown children of Roger Maris, who had come to St. Louis to share in this historic moment. And as fireworks lit up the night-time sky, Sosa, in a great display of sportsmanship, trotted in from right field to exchange bear hugs with Big Mac.

Although Mark had beaten Sosa to the record, the two stars continued dueling for the home run crown until the final weekend of the season, when Mac went yard five times in three games to finish with the almost unbelievable total of 70, four ahead of Sosa. "I can't believe I did it," said Mac with undisguised delight in his accomplishment. "It absolutely blows me away. It's a huge number. I'm proud of what I've been doing with Sammy Sosa. It's been a tremendous ride for me and for him."

MARK McGWIRE

Born: October 1, 1963, in Pomona, California
Height: 6' 5"   Weight: 245
Bats: Right   Throws: Right
Round drafted: First (1984)
Major league seasons: 12

CAREER STATS

AVG.	AB	HITS	HR	RBI	RUNS	SB
.264	5131	1353	457	1130	941	8

SAMMY SOSA

Sammy Sosa has traveled an almost unimaginable distance, from his poverty-stricken childhood in a Dominican town to a lavish penthouse apartment high above Chicago's concrete sidewalks. Born in San Pedro de Macorís, a seaside city in the Dominican Republic, one of the poorest countries in the Caribbean, Sammy early on saw baseball as an escape from the uncertain economic life that would otherwise be awaiting him. Latin America, in general, and the Dominican Republic, specifically, has become a hotbed of baseball activity, feeding players into the big leagues on a regular basis. San Pedro de Macorís, for some unknown reason, is the epicenter of that movement of Latin players to North America, producing more major leaguers than any city its size in the world. Observing the lifestyle that some of those players led served as an early inspiration for Sammy, who used to shine shoes and sell oranges in the streets of San Pedro to help his widowed mother feed her six other children. "I used to see George Bell, Julio Franco, Joaquin Andujar," recalled Sammy. "They

CHICAGO CUBS - OUTFIELDER

built beautiful homes. I remember thinking that it would be nice to live like that."

When he first started playing in neighborhood baseball games, Sammy was so poor that he couldn't even afford a glove, and had to settle for fielding balls with a converted cardboard milk carton. Sammy didn't play any organized ball until he was 14, but by the time he was 16 his power, speed, and intensity had attracted the attention of the major-league scouts who scour Latin America.

"From the first time I saw him, he set himself apart with his aggressiveness and his drive," said Sandy Johnson, who was the Texas Rangers' director of scouting when the team signed Sammy to a minor-league contract in 1986. "He had this fire in his eyes. He was like a young colt out of control. But he was so determined to make it that you couldn't help but notice him."

When Sammy arrived in the United States at age 17, he was a young man from a small Spanish-speaking country, away from his home and family for the first time in his life, trying to learn a difficult trade in a country whose language he knew only slightly. Sammy was also handicapped by the fact that he had played so little organized ball that he hadn't learned the basic ABCs of playing the game.

He had good speed, but he hadn't been taught how to steal or run the bases. He had awesome power, but he was a wild swinger who had only a vague idea of the strike zone. But he was able to use his natural ability and sheer determination to overcome those obstacles and rapidly rise through the Rangers' minor-league system. "We thought he had great potential," said Toronto Blue Jays general manager Gord Ash, who had been tracking Sammy's progress since he was 16. "The ball just made a certain noise whenever he made contact."

The Rangers were also excited about Sammy's prospects and brought him up to Texas early in the 1989 season. But his lack of schooling and discipline as a hitter came back to haunt him against major-league pitching, and the Rangers quickly traded him to the Chicago White Sox. A little more than two years later, after watching Sammy struggle and make little progress as a hitter, the White Sox also gave up on Sammy and dealt him crosstown to the Chicago Cubs.

It wasn't until 1993, his second season at Wrigley Field, when he ripped 33 home runs, that Sammy started rocking the ball and delivering on the promise of his considerable potential. Then he took another step forward in 1994, a season shortened by a bitter labor dispute, compiling a .300 average and rapping 25 home runs in only 105 games. Sammy settled into a groove over the next three seasons, averaging better than 37 home runs and

112 RBIs a year, numbers that earned him a spot on the 1995 National League All-Star Team and confirmed him as one of the most productive hitters in the league. He'd also become, in 1993, the first Cubbie to hit 30 homers and steal 30 bases in the same season, a feat that he repeated in 1995. Life had become very sweet for Sammy, who had signed a four-year, $42 million contract, but neither he nor anyone else had any idea of how much better it was about to become.

Surprisingly, Sammy started the 1998 season slowly, collecting only 13 home runs by the end of May, 14 less than major-league leader Mark McGwire. But in June, Sammy suddenly struck with unprecedented consistency, whacking 20 big flies in June, more home runs than any player had hit in any month in big-league history. "I've seen a lot of things in this game, but I've never seen anything like *this*," said Cubs first baseman Mark Grace. Just like that, Sammy found himself in the midst of the Great Race, running to challenge the single-season mark of 61, which Roger Maris had set 37 years earlier.

Sammy headed into the second half of the season with 33 homers, two behind Ken Griffey, Jr., who would eventually fade from contention, and four behind McGwire, with whom Sammy would contend until the season's final games. Although

Sammy maintained that he wasn't trying to hit home runs, merely trying to help the Cubs make it into the playoffs, he not only accomplished his goal but also managed to join McGwire in creating the most exciting record chase in sports history.

Although Sammy wound up blasting his sixty-second home run five days after Big Mac had broken the tape and finished with 66 dingers, nothing that anyone else did could diminish what Sammy had accomplished. "It's been a beautiful year," said Sammy, who led the majors with 158 RBIs, the fourth highest total in National League history, and outran Mac for the league's MVP trophy. "No one is going to forget 1998."

SAMMY SOSA

Born: November 12, 1968, in San Pedro de
      Macorís, Dominican Republic
Height: 6' 0"   Weight: 210
Bats: Right   Throws: Right
Not drafted
Major league seasons: 9+

CAREER STATS

AVG.	AB	HITS	HR	RBI	RUNS	SB
.264	4664	1233	273	800	727	217

KEN GRIFFEY, JR.

Like Michael Jordan, Ken Griffey, Jr., is such a gifted athlete that he's sometimes referred to as the Natural. Even when he was just a little boy, Junior was already displaying the spectacular abilities that stamped him as something special. He started his Little League career by lashing 11 home runs in his first six games, and he was such a dominant pitcher that opposing players would go to the plate in tears. "You're better than I am," Junior was told by his dad, Ken Griffey, Sr., who was in the midst of a nineteen-year major-league career.

Junior also displayed his enormous skills at Cincinnati's Moeller High School, where he became an authentic prep school legend for his play as a wide receiver on the football team, as well as for what he did on the baseball diamond. "He could have been just as good at football as he is at baseball if he stuck with it," said Scott Schaffner, who was the team's quarterback. "He was that good."

And Griffey was so good at baseball that he hit .400 in each of his four seasons at Moeller. "There

KEN GRIFFEY, JR.

SEATTLE MARINERS - OUTFIELDER

17

were times he'd hit a ball so far, it was like a golf ball," recalled Schaffner, who played third base for Moeller's baseball team. "We played on a field with no fence. You'd see outfielders five hundred feet back, and he'd still pop it over their heads."

Junior had shown such vast potential that the Seattle Mariners, who owned the number one overall pick in the 1987 draft, selected him without a second of hesitation. Almost before the ink had dried on his first professional contract, Junior was already being compared with Darryl Strawberry, at the time an All-Star outfielder, who had played a pivotal role in the New York Mets' capture of the 1986 World Series. "Kenny is similar to Darryl in that he is tall, strong, and has a powerful stroke," said Roger Jongewaard, who was Seattle's director of scouting. "Defensively, Kenny is quicker than Darryl and covers more ground. With his gifts, Kenny could also become an All-Star regular."

Three years later, and playing in only his second season in the big leagues, Junior made Jongewaard seem like a prophet when he became the second-youngest player ever to start in a major-league All-Star game. Junior did it at the plate, posting a .300 average, and he also did it in the field, where his dazzling defensive work prompted coaches and managers to award him a Gold Glove as the top-fielding center fielder in the American League.

"Every game you know you're going to see some-thing you'll have trouble believing," said former teammate Scott Bradley. "He never ceases to amaze me. He makes what we call 'You've got to be kidding catches' all the time."

But for the Griffey clan, the most memorable moments of the 1990 season occurred after Senior came out of retirement and became Junior's team-mate for the final month of the season. "I was so nervous, it was like being a rookie again," said Senior, half of the only father and son team ever to play in a major-league game together. "Of all the things that have happened to me—the World Series, the All-Star games, everything—this is number one. This is the best thing that's ever happened to me."

Playing alongside his son also allowed the senior Griffey to admire just how great a fielder Junior had become. "I'm in awe of him, too," the senior Griffey told reporters after his son had made one of his routine "Play of the Day" grabs. "I might have made two or three great grabs in my entire career, but he makes them nearly all the time. It's like he has rockets in his feet and a magnet in his glove."

Although Junior quickly established himself as a perennial All-Star and a virtually automatic Gold Glove selection, he didn't become a big-time slugger until his fifth season, when he bopped 45, one behind the 1993 major-league coleaders Juan

Gonzalez, the Texas Rangers' right fielder, and Barry Bonds, the gifted left fielder for the San Francisco Giants. Included in Junior's total was one torrid stretch in which he became only the third player to whack home runs in eight straight games. According to Erik Hanson, who was a teammate of Junior's, the end of the streak saved Seattle's ballpark. "If he had hit another one, the roof would have come off, and we'd have an outdoor stadium. That's how loud the place was getting."

While Junior insists that he's not a home run hitter, he's been the American League leader in three of the last five seasons, while becoming the youngest player in major-league history to clock 350 career dingers. "He has the perfect home run swing," asserts Hall of Famer Joe Morgan, who has become one of the best baseball analysts on or off the tube. "He has a slight uppercut, great bat speed, and great strength. Plus, he just keeps getting better."

Junior's numbers, especially over the past three seasons, support Morgan's claim and puts him in the company of some of the game's all-time greats. In that time, Junior has averaged just under 54 dingers a season, and joined Babe Ruth and Lou Gehrig as the only players ever to drive in 140 runs in three successive seasons. In his career, Junior, who was a unanimous choice as the American League's 1997 MVP, has averaged over 100 RBIs a season and become the fourth youngest player to drive in a thousand runs.

His spectacular play and pleasant personality have made Junior a great favorite with fans, who have voted him in as an All-Star Game starter for nine straight seasons. And he receives just as much respect and appreciation from the league's coaches and managers, who have awarded him nine straight Gold Gloves for his exquisite fielding, as well as five Silver Slugger Awards as the best-hitting center fielder in the AL. "I've played with some great players, but he is, bar none, the best I've ever played with," said former teammate, Paul Sorrento. "He's the best I've ever seen."

KEN GRIFFEY, JR.

Born: November 21, 1969, in Donora,
      Pennsylvania
Height: 6' 3"   Weight: 205
Bats: Left   Throws: Left
Round drafted: First (1987)
Major league seasons: 10

CAREER STATS

AVG.	AB	HITS	HR	RBI	RUNS	SB
.300	5226	1569	350	1018	940	143

DEREK JETER

Derek Jeter began learning the game of baseball and the joy of playing it from watching his father, a former college shortstop, play softball on the playgrounds of Kalamazoo, Michigan. When Derek was old enough to join a Little League team, he wanted to play shortstop, just like his dad. But the team's coach, who just happened to be his father, decided to put another boy at short and play Derek at second. "I told him not to worry about things he couldn't control and just enjoy himself," recalled Charles Jeter, advice which his son has carried with him throughout his life.

Derek also learned other lessons as the child of an African-American father and a Caucasian mother. As a youngster, Derek was made uncomfortable by all the people who would stare at the relative oddity of seeing a biracial couple. "It bothered me when I was growing up," said Derek, who has always had a racially diverse group of friends. "But I don't think about it anymore. I wouldn't change a thing. I have the best of both worlds. Fans, though, always want to know what I am. I don't have a

DEREK JETER

NEW YORK YANKEES - SHORTSTOP

problem with that. People are curious. If you're curious, you can ask."

One place that Derek never had too much trouble was the baseball diamond, where his natural talent, enthusiasm, and hard work came together to produce mostly spectacular results. "Some people say that Derek is lucky," said Dan Hinga, who coached one of the summer league teams on which Derek played as a teenager. "Well, he's fortunate that he's 6′ 3″ and has long arms and legs. But he worked his rear end off. He would arrive early for games and take grounders, and after games, he would stand out there and take grounders as long as there was somebody to hit balls to him."

All that hard work helped Derek hit a gaudy .557 as a junior at Kalamazoo's Central High School. Then he closed out his school career by hitting .508 while driving in 23 runs in 23 games and going 12 for 12 in steal attempts. Derek's play was so spectacular that he was named the 1992 High School Player of the Year by the American Baseball Coaches Association, and he showed so much potential that the New York Yankees made the lanky young shortstop their first pick in the June draft. Derek struggled in the field and at the plate in his first season of professional ball, but in 1993, playing with Class A Greensboro, he lifted his play several notches and was voted the Most Outstanding Major

League Prospect of the year by the South Atlantic League managers.

Derek then made a major move up the Yanks' organization chart the following year, leapfrogging all the way from Class A to Triple A, while posting a blended .344 average and 50 stolen bases. After that awesome performance, which prompted *Baseball America* to name him Minor League Player of the Year, and a full season at Triple A, during which he batted .317, Derek knew he'd get the chance to open the 1996 season in the Big Apple. Although there were some people in the Yankees organization who weren't convinced that Derek was ready to anchor the infield of a championship-caliber team, manager Joe Torre thought otherwise.

Derek began repaying Torre's vote of confidence with a picture-perfect opening day that included a home run and a spectacular over-the-shoulder grab. Although he made his share of rookie mistakes, Derek impressed with his willingness to accept criticism and learn from it. After he had broken a cardinal baserunning rule by making the third out at third base, instead of trying to duck away from Torre, Derek went over to his manager to acknowledge the mistake. "That told me he's not afraid to accept responsibility," said Torre. "That's a sign of responsibility."

"When you make a mistake, you should own up to it, learn from it, and move on," said Derek, who learned so well that he went on to post a .314 average on his way to becoming only the fifth unanimous choice as the American League Rookie of the Year before playing a key role in the Yankees' winning of the 1996 World Series. "I went over to Joe because I knew he'd want to make sure I'd learned my lesson.

"I'm not afraid of failure. If you are, you can't be successful. So I'm not going to think negatively. When you do that, you fail before you even get started. I'm going to think positively."

Derek continued his superior play in 1997, finishing among the league leaders in hits, runs, triples, and stolen bases, while joining Hall of Famer Joe DiMaggio as the only two Yankees ever to score 100 runs in each of their first two seasons. Any thoughts that Derek might become a legend in his own mind were dispelled by his decision to buy a house in Tampa, Florida, so that he could spend his time during off-seasons working out at the Yankees' training complex. "Baseball is a real humbling sport," explained Derek. "One day you're on top and the next day you're not. I'm enjoying this now, but I don't think you have to worry about me getting a big head. Until you hit 1.000 and make no errors, you always have something to improve upon."

His efforts and his attitude paid off handsomely in 1998, as Derek set career highs in most offensive categories, including home runs, batting average, and stolen bases, while cutting his errors in half. Named to his first All-Star Game, Derek also helped spark the Yankees to their second World Series win in his three seasons, and finished third in the voting for the American League MVP Award. "He's our MVP," said Torre, after surveying a world championship team which included the likes of Paul O'Neill and Bernie Williams, the American League batting champion. "And it's no accident. Nobody works harder than Derek does."

DEREK JETER

Born: June 26, 1974, in Pequannock, New Jersey
Height: 6' 3"   Weight: 185
Bats: Right   Throws: Right
Round drafted: First (1992)
Major league seasons: 3

CAREER STATS

AVG.	AB	HITS	HR	RBI	RUNS	SB
.308	1910	588	39	239	352	67

BARRY SANDERS

Barry Sanders has been bringing fans to their feet and defenders to their knees ever since he ran for an 80-yard touchdown on his first carry in a Pee-Wee League game. "He makes you stand on your toes every time he touches the ball," said Wayne Fontes, the former Detroit Lions head coach who had a sideline view of Barry's first eight years in the NFL. "You watch because you feel like something big is going to happen."

Ironically, Barry almost missed his chance to become one of the greatest running backs in football history because his high school coach thought that he was too small to play the position. It wasn't until the sixth game of his senior year at North High School in Wichita, Kansas, that Barry was finally given the chance to carry the ball. But he responded to the opportunity with breathtaking style, streaking for 274 yards in his first game, and finishing his short season with 1,417 yards, a new city of Wichita rushing record.

Although Barry was born with the gift of speed and the ability to change direction with the quickness

BARRY SANDERS

DETROIT LIONS - RUNNING BACK

29

of the Roadrunner, what has set him apart from a lot of other people who are born with great talent is his extraordinary work ethic. Even when he was being bypassed by his high school coach, Barry spent hours a day lifting weights and running sprints, building up his strength and his stamina. "When I was young someone told me, 'You are what you do every day,'" said Barry. "It made me realize that I had to work every day or time would pass me by."

But instead of concentrating on Barry's ability and work habits, major college football programs focused on his height and decided that he wasn't worth a scholarship. "It's amazing to me how much attention coaches pay to size instead of talent," said Barry, who wound up accepting a scholarship to Oklahoma State University. "The fact that most of the big schools ignored me didn't discourage me. It gave me the incentive to show them that it's not all about size."

During his first two years at OSU, Barry played behind All-American running back Thurman Thomas, who would go on to become an All-Pro with the Buffalo Bills. While Barry waited his turn to become the featured back, he made a major contribution on special teams in his sophomore season with the OSU Cowboys, leading the nation in kickoff returns and finishing second in punt returns. Barry also put in major hours in the weight room, building up his body and strengthening his legs so that he'd be ready to carry the load when his time came.

All that work paid off like a lottery jackpot in his junior year, as Barry recorded what may be the single greatest season that any college running back has ever posted. In that amazing 1988 season, Barry set 13 NCAA records, including single-season marks for rushing yards (2,628) and touchdowns scored (39), and was an easy winner of the Heisman Trophy as the best college football player in the nation.

The Detroit Lions grabbed Barry with the third overall pick of the 1989 draft, and he immediately showed that he was up to the challenge by piling up an NFC-high 1,470 yards, only 10 behind the league leader, Christian Okoye. Barry, who was named the NFL's Offensive Rookie of the Year, actually had a chance to pass Okoye in the closing minutes of the season, but since the Lions already had an insurmountable lead in the game, he just stood on the sidelines and cheered for his backup. "He's not only the best running back I've ever seen," said Wayne Fontes. "He's also the best person I've ever met."

The following year Barry did win the NFL rushing title, the first of four that he's captured, and he also caught the eye of the great Walter Payton, who had terrorized opposing defenses for 13 seasons before leaving the game as the NFL's career rushing and total yardage leader. "I don't know if I was ever *that* good," said Payton, who retired from the Chicago Bears in 1987 after having romped for 16,726 rushing yards and 21,803 total yards. Now, after 10 seasons of unparalleled play, Barry, who has run for 15,269 yards and racked up 18,308 total yards, is on target to unseat Payton as the game's all-time leading rusher by the end of the 1999 season, and will likely surpass Payton's total yardage mark by the end of the 2000 season.

He already holds a lion's share of NFL records, including most 150-yard rushing games (25); consecutive 100-yard rushing games (14); and consecutive 1,000-yard seasons (10 and counting). And Barry, who in 1997 became only the third back in league history to rush for over 2,000 yards, is a cinch to add other lines into the NFL record book before he rides off into the sunset. But even if he was to hang up his spikes today, Barry's place in football history would already be secure, with his startling runs captured on tape for future generations to marvel at. "Anytime he has the ball, it's a highlight reel," said television analyst Marcus Allen, who racked up 17,648 total yards in his own storied career. "Barry Sanders is the most dangerous player in the game and the most fun to watch. He's just remarkable."

BARRY SANDERS

Born: July 16, 1968, in Wichita, Kansas
Height: 5' 8"   Weight: 203
College: Oklahoma State
Round drafted: First (1989)
NFL seasons: 10

CAREER STATS

Rushing		Receiving		
Yards	Avg.	No.	Yards	TD
15,269	5.0	352	2,921	109

BRETT FAVRE

Brett Favre knew he had found his calling after moving from wide receiver to quarterback during his first organized football game. "I was switched to quarterback, and it was like a jamboree," said Brett, who was in the fifth grade and liked to pretend that he was Archie Manning, the quarterback of the New Orleans Saints. "I had like three touchdown passes, and ran for maybe three more, and I said, 'This is for me.'"

Despite going on to become a four-year starter at Hancock North Central High School in the small town of Kiln, Mississippi, Brett's career almost came to an abrupt end because he didn't attract the interest of a single college coach. The problem was that the coach of the team, Brett's dad, Irvin, used a run-oriented offense in which Brett threw only 55 passes—mostly short-range—in his four-year stint. And when a recruiter from the University of Southern Mississippi finally did show up in Kiln, it seemed like a wasted trip, because when he looked at game tapes what he mostly saw was Brett handing the ball off with numbing regularity. But on the

BRETT FAVRE

GREEN BAY PACKERS - QUARTERBACK

35

last tape, there was one pass that was so stunning that it still remains imbedded in the memory of the recruiter, Mark McHale.

"First he play-faked and rolled out to the right hash mark, just about midfield," recalled McHale, as though he were watching the play on a private rerun machine. "Then he stopped, planted his feet, and threw the ball into the end zone with *smoke* coming off it. I mean *flames* are shooting out, and it drills this little receiver for a touchdown and near kills the kid."

McHale's enthusiasm was enough to get Brett's name on the list of possible USM recruits, but it was at the bottom of a quarterback wish list with 15 other names above it. It was only after the other prospective signal callers either accepted scholarships to other schools, or were whittled off the list for other reasons, that Brett was offered the final scholarship that USM handed out in 1982. "I know that I received the scholarship only because the ball took a lot of funny bounces," said Brett. "And I didn't really think I was a good enough passer when I went up there."

Although Brett had arrived on campus by default and was unsure of his own abilities, by the time he left, he owned nearly every passing line in the USM record book. "We got lucky," admitted former USM head coach Curly Hallman, who had watched Brett work his way into the top rank of college quarter-backs. "Let's face it, we ended up finding a four-year starter from a place that's kind of like *The Dukes of Hazzard*, minus the demolition derby."

Selected by Atlanta in the second round of the 1991 draft, Brett spent his rookie year in the NFL shackled to the bench as the Falcons' third-string quarterback. But Ron Wolf, the Packers' cagey general manager, believing that Brett could become a franchise quarterback, swapped his number one pick in the 1992 draft to bring Brett to Green Bay. "He had a toughness and a competitiveness that we liked a lot, but the biggest attribute he possesses is leadership," said Wolf. "He just has that unex-plainable something."

But halfway into his third season in Green Bay, Brett had only delivered short flashes of brilliance surrounded by long stretches of erratic play and poor decision making. "I thought if I had one more bad game, I was gone," said Brett. But former Packers head coach Mike Holmgren, sensing that Brett was frazzled and knowing that he had the tools for greatness, sat his struggling quarterback down and told him, "We're joined at the hip. Either we go to the top of the mountain together or we're both going to wind up on the dumpster."

Brett, responding to the vote of confidence as though he'd been thrown a lifeline, burned up the league by throwing for 24 touchdowns and only seven interceptions in the final nine games of the 1994 season. "Now I feel like I really am one of the best quarterbacks in the league," said Brett, who totaled an NFL-best 33 scoring strikes. Brett backed up those words the following season by throwing for an NFC-record 38 TD passes and being named the NFL's Most Valuable Player. "Individual honors are nice, but I know that quarterbacks are measured for greatness by winning Super Bowls," said Brett. "There's no doubt that before my career's over, I'm going to win a Super Bowl for Green Bay."

Which is exactly what Favre did, after topping his own NFC record by throwing 39 scoring strikes and leading the Packers to a 13-3 record and a second successive division title. Favre's spectacular play also earned him a second MVP Award, allowing him to join Joe Montana, Steve Young, and Hall of Famers Jim Brown and Johnny Unitas, as the only two-time winners. Then Favre capped off his spectacular season by leading Green Bay to a 35–21 win over the New England Patriots in Super Bowl XXXI. "I can't see any flaws in him," said Bobby Bethard, the general manager of the San Diego Chargers. "He can and will run and he can throw on the run. He makes all the plays, and he's developed such consistency. If there's a flaw, I don't see it."

Brett has continued his extraordinary level of play, earning an unprecedented third MVP trophy in 1997, while leading the league in passing yards and completion percentage in 1998. Brett also holds virtually every Packers passing record and owns the third-best career passing record in NFL history. But there's still a lot of little boy left in him. "Even though I've finally made it, sometimes I still have to pinch myself when I think there's a little kid running around somewhere saying, 'I'm Brett Favre.'"

BRETT FAVRE

Born: October 10, 1969, in Gulfport, Mississippi
Height: 6' 2"   Weight: 230
College: Southern Mississippi
Round Drafted: Second (1991)
NFL seasons: 8

CAREER STATS

ATT.	COMP.	YDS.	TD	INT.
3,757	2,318	26,803	213	118

TERRELL DAVIS

The emergence of Terrell Davis as a full-blown NFL superstar is as unlikely as the plot of the dopiest Hollywood movie ever made. Prior to joining the Denver Broncos as an unheralded sixth-round selection in the 1995 draft, Terrell's first and only touch of stardom had occurred when he averaged 15 yards per carry and three touchdowns a game for his San Diego, California, Pop Warner League team. But when his father died while Terrell was in ninth grade, he crawled into a shell and stopped playing football until his junior year at Lincoln High School. The team had so many high-quality running backs, however, that Terrell had to scramble and switch positions to find a place to play.

"He wanted to be a running back, but we had kids who ran the hundred in 10.5, and we didn't think Terrell was fast enough to get the job done," recalled Lincoln head coach Tony Jackson. "Then he said he wanted to be a linebacker, but we were loaded there, too. So we put him at nose guard, where we needed some help, and he also played fullback, mostly as a blocker."

TERRELL DAVIS

DENVER BRONCOS - RUNNING BACK

The memory of Terrell's bone-crunching blocks still brings a smile to his coach's face. "I'll never forget the Point Loma game," said Jackson, shaking his head. "Their linebackers were actually stepping out of the way, so that Terrell couldn't lay a hit on them. Linebackers are usually the toughest guys on the team, but they didn't want any part of him."

But when not even one college football team offered him a scholarship, it seemed as though Terrell's football-playing days had come to a halt. "I have always been in situations where things didn't look good, where I couldn't see a light at the end of a tunnel," explained Terrell. "I figured football was over for me when I finished high school. Same with college. I was never a blue-chipper. I was never the best. I can't really explain what's happened. But all those experiences made me mentally tougher, taught me that whatever doesn't kill you makes you stronger."

Luckily, Terrell finally did receive a last-minute scholarship to Long Beach State, but only with the strong urgings of his older half brother, Reggie Webb, who was a tailback on the team. Terrell played in virtual obscurity at LBS, carrying the ball only 55 times during his one year of action before transferring to the University of Georgia because Long Beach State dropped football. During his first year at Georgia, Terrell played behind Garrison

Hearst, the great running back of the San Francisco 49ers, who finished third in the voting for the 1992 Heisman Trophy. After Hearst left for the NFL in 1993, Terrell took over as the Bulldogs' featured back, but never received the confidence of his head coach, Ray Goff. Plagued by injuries for most of his senior year and bad-mouthed by Goff, Terrell was drafted low, and neither he nor the Broncos gave him much of a chance of making it past training camp. "I was thinking, 'When you get drafted this late, all you are is camp meat,'" recalled Terrell, who was the twenty-second running back selected in 1995. But Terrell surprised everybody with his running, his attitude and his intelligence. "You tell Terrell something once, he gets it," said Denver running backs coach Bobby Turner. "Tell him twice, he *owns* it.'

By the start of the season, Terrell also owned the Broncos' starting running back job, and by the end of his rookie year, after rampaging for 1,117 yards rushing, he had become the lowest-drafted running back ever to rush for a thousand yards in a season. "There isn't an area of his game that isn't strong," said Denver head coach Mike Shanahan, citing Terrell's soft hands, which had pulled in 49 passes, and his devastating blocking.

Terrell showed that he wasn't a one-year wonder by rushing for an AFC-best 1,538 yards in 1996, and finishing as the NFL runner-up to Barry Sanders in both rushing yards and total yards from scrimmage. Although Terrell is not especially big, he's a powerful runner with breakaway speed and great field vision that allows him to find little cracks to run through. And once he's past the line of scrimmage, it's usually a mismatch in Terrell's favor. "You just don't want to let him get into the secondary," said Atlanta Falcons defensive coordinator Rich Brooks.

But no one found a way to stop Terrell, who erupted for 1,750 rushing yards in 1997, once again topping the AFC in rushing and becoming the fourth fastest in league history to rush for 4,000 yards in a career. Then Terrell put the cherry on his season by rushing for 157 yards and earning game MVP honors for leading the Broncos to a 31–24 win against the Green Bay Packers in Super Bowl XXXII. "It's hard to even believe I could be here in this situation," said Terrell, who was sidelined for most of the second quarter with an excruciating migraine headache. "But to win MVP? *No way*! I'm back to where I used to be in Pop Warner."

Just when it seemed that the script couldn't get any better, Terrell tore through opposing defenses for 2,008 yards in 1998, becoming only the fourth player in league history to rush for 2,000, and was named the NFL's MVP. Terrell continued his dominant running in the playoffs, keying the

Broncos run to a second Super Bowl win with a trio of 100-yard games. "He played a heck of a game," said Atlanta head coach Dan Reeves, after Denver had demolished the Falcons on Super Sunday. "I've never seen anybody break so many tackles."

Believe it or not, there it is—*The Impossible Journey: The Terrell Davis Story.*

TERRELL DAVIS

Born: October 28, 1972, in San Diego, California
Height: 5' 11"   Weight: 205 pounds
College: Long Beach State and Georgia
Round drafted: Sixth   (1995)
NFL seasons: 4

CAREER STATS

Rushing		Receiving		
Yards	Avg.	No.	Yards	TD
6,413	4.8	152	1,181	61

ERIC LINDROS

By the time he was sixteen, every hockey fan in Canada knew that Eric Lindros was the most exceptional young player to appear on the scene since Mario Lemieux had emerged a decade earlier. "Eric is the best sixteen-year-old player I've ever seen," claimed Bobby Clarke, a Hall-of-Fame center who had led the Philadelphia Flyers to back-to-back Stanley Cup triumphs in 1974 and 1975 before taking over as the team's general manager. "He could play in the NHL right now."

Although Eric was too young to play in the NHL, he did put up monster numbers in his only full season with the Oshawa Generals of the Ontario Hockey League, scoring 71 goals and totaling 149 points in only 57 games. Eric's performance catapulted the Generals to victory in the Memorial Cup, the tournament that brings together the best junior hockey teams in Canada. Named the 1991 Player of the Year in the Canadian Hockey League, which is given to the top performer from among the three major Junior Leagues in Canada, Eric was the unrivaled choice as the top player in the NHL

ERIC LINDROS

PHILADELPHIA FLYERS - CENTER

47

Entry Draft. But his road to the pros was delayed for a year because he took the unprecedented step of refusing to sign with the Quebec Nordiques, the team that had drafted him. (The Nordiques have since moved to Colorado and changed their name to the Avalanche.)

Eric, who speaks only English, may not have wanted to play for the Nordiques because Quebec is a part of French-speaking Canada, or because of reasonable fears that a majority of the people of Quebec would vote to secede from the English-speaking provinces of Canada. But the only public reason that Eric offered was an extreme dislike of the team's former owner, Marcel Aubut. "I had no respect for him," recalled Eric. "He didn't treat his players well. He told me that if went to Quebec, I'd be a god. To be quite honest with you, I don't want to be a god."

While Eric sat out the 1991–92 NHL season he played for the Canadian National Junior Team and the Canadian Olympic Team, as well as Team Canada, a collection of NHL all-stars who were chosen to represent their country against other international squads in the Canada Cup Tournament. Playing with and against the greatest players in the world, Eric scored three goals in eight games and made a vivid impression on the Great One. "He's going to carry the NHL," promised Wayne Gretzky.

Eric finally got his chance to start living up to that high praise during the 1992–93 season, after Aubut had given up on signing him and traded his rights to the Philadelphia Flyers for six players, including Peter Forsberg, a pair of first-round draft choices, *and* $15 million. In only his fourth game in the league, Eric had to square off against the Nordiques in front of a very loud and angry capacity crowd in Quebec. The fans showed their anger by waving nasty banners and stupidly throwing objects onto the ice. Included in their barrage was a large amount of baby bottles and pacifiers, the fans' way of expressing their belief that Eric had been babied by his parents. Eric answered their inane actions by scoring a pair of goals and laughing at their antics. "I got a few gifts," said Eric, who went on to score a Flyers rookie-record 41 goals despite being side-lined for 21 games. "If I have a child, I won't have to buy any pacifiers."

Injuries also cut into Eric's playing time during the 1993–94 season, limiting the big center to only 65 games. But he still made his large presence felt, becoming one of the most feared checkers in the league, while scoring 97 points, eleventh-best in the NHL. "There are some defensemen in this league who are so afraid of Eric they just get out of his way," noted Chicago Blackhawks star defenseman Chris Chelios. Although Eric was injury-free the following year, a dispute between the players and owners cut nearly half the games out of the 1994–95 schedule. But once play started, Eric turned nearly every game into a highlight tape, tying Jaromir Jagr with a league-leading 70 points and capturing the Hart Memorial Trophy as the league's MVP. "It's almost unfair," said Flyers goalie, Ron Hextall. "There's no one who can physically challenge him. He's so big and strong and skilled, he can hurt you in so many ways."

Eric continued to score points at a torrid pace over the following three seasons, becoming the fifth-fastest player to score 500 points. But his play in four straight postseason appearances was less than stellar, prompting Flyers general manager Bobby Clarke to openly criticize Eric for not having led Philadelphia to a Stanley Cup championship. "He's not a kid anymore," said Clarke during the summer of 1998. "It's time. If he wants to be paid like one of the top players in the game, then he needs to play like one."

Stung by Clarke's challenge, Eric has responded to the criticism by playing the best hockey of his life during the first two-thirds of the 1998–99 season. Eric was once again dueling Jagr for the scoring title, and he also led the Flyers to the top of the Eastern Conference standings, putting them on target for a serious run at Lord Stanley's Cup. "He's always been a great talent," conceded Clarke. "Now he's applying it every game and every day at practice. I think he's playing like the best player in the league."

ERIC LINDROS

Born: February 28, 1973, in London, Ontario, Canada
Height: 6' 4"   Weight: 236
Round drafted: First (1991)
NHL seasons: 6

CAREER STATS

GAMES	GOALS	ASSISTS	POINTS
360	223	284	507

All stats through the 1997–98 season.

MICHAEL JORDAN

The greatness that Michael Jordan created on the basketball court grew out of his failures. Instead of letting failure defeat him, as so many other people do, Michael used his intelligence, his unsurpassed work ethic, and his iron will to uncover every talent that he possessed and become the greatest basketball player who ever lived. Michael's competitive drive and intensity are so compelling that, as one of his former college team-mates said, "It's really almost like being burned."

Michael's first failures came against his older brother, Larry, who used to whip him in the one-on-one games they played on their backyard court in Wilmington, North Carolina. "Larry always used to beat me," remembered Michael, who just dug in his heels and worked that much harder to keep up with his brother. "He's got all the dunks and some three-sixties and most of the same stuff I have. And he's only five-seven. He's my inspiration."

But losing to Larry in their private backyard games was a lot easier to take than being cut from the varsity team in his sophomore year at Laney High

MICHAEL JORDAN

CHICAGO BULLS - GUARD

53

School. "It was embarrassing not to make the team," admits Michael, who used his humiliation as a springboard to becoming a starter the following year, and a high school All-American as a senior. "Whenever I worked out, got tired, and thought about stopping, I'd close my eyes and see those lists without my name on them. That was all I needed to get going again."

Michael's next stop was the University of North Carolina, where in his freshman year he made one of the most memorable shots in NCAA Finals history, a fifteen-foot jumper with 15 seconds left to play that lifted the Tar Heels to the 1982 NCAA Championship. Although Michael was playing in a lineup that included All-American and future NBA star James Worthy, former UNC coach Dean Smith didn't hesitate to put the ball in his freshman's hands. "To me, the most significant thing about that shot was that they had James Worthy, who was absolutely killing us," remembered former Georgetown coach John Thompson. "But they went to Michael."

Michael continued to expand his game offensively and defensively during his three-year stay at UNC, and was named *The Sporting News* College Player of the Year after both his sophomore and junior seasons. Then Michael, who was the third player taken in the 1984 NBA draft, led a squad of college all-stars to a gold medal at the Summer Olympics.

"He's not human," cried an opposing coach. "He's a rubber man."

Michael then began his fabled career with the Chicago Bulls, blazing across the NBA like a supernova, establishing himself as the game's brightest star and its fiercest competitor. Michael's high-flying play earned him Rookie of the Year honors for the 1984–85 season, and, a year later, after missing 62 games with a broken foot, Air Jordan returned to light up the Boston Celtics for an NBA playoff-record 63 points. "He's the most awesome player in the NBA," said ex-Celtic great Larry Bird.

The following year Michael won his first NBA scoring title, averaging 37.1 points per game, and became the first player to record 200 steals and 100 blocks in a season. While his critics conceded that Michael was the greatest *talent* in the game, he couldn't be considered a truly great *player*, they maintained, until he'd led the Bulls to an NBA championship. That was a mountain that Michael tried and failed to climb in each of his first six seasons, but the failures only made him work harder, pushing him to add additional elements to his game.

The breakthrough for Michael came in his seventh season, when he led the Bulls over Magic Johnson and the Los Angeles Lakers in the NBA Finals. Then he broke down in tears while hugging the championship trophy. "All the struggles, all the people saying, 'He's not going to win,' all those little doubts you have about yourself, you have to put them aside and tell yourself, 'I am a winner, I am going to win,'" said Michael, who was named MVP of the regular season and the finals. "And then when you do it, well, it's just amazing."

Michael continued to win and amaze everyone who ever saw him play, thrilling people with his athleticism and leading the Bulls to three straight NBA titles. "Michael is the greatest player I've ever seen," said Lakers executive Jerry West, who was one of the NBA's all-time great players. "He's the best offensive player I've ever seen, and his defense is second to none."

After temporarily retiring for eighteen months, Michael returned to basketball at the tail end of the 1984–95 schedule, then came back the following season and led the Bulls to another trio of championships. In the final few minutes of what would turn out to be his last game in the NBA, Michael simply took control of the outcome, making a critical steal and scoring his team's final eight points. Michael's game-winning shot was a thing of beauty—a hard drive, a crossover dribble that left his defender defenseless, and then the jump shot that caught nothing but net. "I didn't think he could cap what he did in last year's playoffs, but I think he just topped it," said Phil Jackson, who was the Bulls coach. "It was the best performance you've seen from Michael in a critical game of a series."

By the time Michael retired from the game prior to the start of the 1999 season, he had won 10 scoring titles, the last of which made him, at 35, the oldest player ever to win an NBA scoring crown. He had also been named to the All-NBA First Team 10 times, and to the All-NBA Defensive Team nine times. He was the league's regular-season MVP five times, and the finals MVP six times. He had become, by all measures, the greatest and most captivating player to ever play the game. "He was Michelangelo in baggy shorts," said Phil Jackson. "A player with such a rich imagination he transformed the game into a work of art."

MICHAEL JORDAN

Born: February 17, 1963, in Brooklyn, New York
Height: 6' 6"   Weight: 216
College: North Carolina
Round drafted: First (1984)
NBA seasons: 13

CAREER STATS (per game average)

Points	Assists	Rebounds	Steals	Blocks
31.5	5.4	6.3	2.5	0.9

SHAQUILLE O'NEAL

It's hard to imagine a time when Shaquille O'Neal wasn't delivering rim-rattling slam dunks, but when he was 13 years old and had already grown to be 6' 6", Shaq couldn't elevate high enough to dunk the ball. One day, after lots of practicing, Shaq finally managed to jam, and ran over to share the good news with his friends. "They didn't think I could jump over a pencil," said Shaq, recalling the teasing that he took. But when he tried to show off his new skill to his friends, he missed one dunk after another. After a while they just left the court, laughing and teasing, "You can't dunk, man."

By the time he was 16, though, Shaq was dunking with authority, and had become a prep school superstar, averaging 39 points per game while leading San Antonio's Cole High School to a 36-0 record and the Texas State championship. Shaq's spectacular play earned him a scholarship to Louisiana State University, where his presence was supposed to guarantee at least one NCAA Championship banner for the LSU Tigers. But the good times never did roll in Baton Rouge, and Shaq

SHAQUILLE O'NEAL

LOS ANGELES LAKERS - CENTER

was never able to lead the Tigers deep into March Madness in any of his three years at LSU. "We were supposed to win every game," recalled Shaq. "But every game turned into a challenge."

Although Shaq wasn't able to carry the Tigers to a title, he was named the Associated Press College Basketball Player of the Year as a sophomore. Shaq was also a consensus All-American in each of his last two seasons at LSU. "He's the closest thing to me that I've ever seen in college ball," said Wilt Chamberlain, generally considered to be, along with Bill Russell, one of the two greatest centers of all time.

"He's a dominant player at both ends of the court," raved Boston Celtics coach Rick Pitino, who at the time was coaching against Shaq at the University of Kentucky. "He's simply the best college player in America. The NBA team that gets him will get an all-star, an immediate impact player."

Shaq, who was taken by the Orlando Magic as the number one overall pick in the 1992 NBA draft, supported Pitino's contention, becoming the first rookie in league history to be named NBA Player of the Week in the first week of a season. And he continued to shine throughout the season, becoming the first rookie to earn an All-Star game start since Michael Jordan had turned the trick in 1985, and finishing among the league leaders in rebounding, shot-blocking, field goal percentage, and scoring. "In all my years, I've never seen a package of talent like this," said veteran center Greg Kite, who watched Shaq become the runaway winner of the 1993 Rookie of the Year award. "Patrick Ewing has a lot of strength, and David Robinson is really quick, but nobody combines the strength and quickness that Shaq has."

Although the awards and praise came pouring in like a summer storm, there wasn't any danger that Shaq was going to sit home staring at his trophy case and reading his press clippings. "That's not me," said Shaq, whose commitment to excellence, and popularity with fans around the country enabled him to become an All-Star game starter in each of his four seasons with Orlando, including 1995, when he led the league in scoring and the Magic into the NBA Finals, where they were swept away by Hakeem Olajuwon and the Houston Rockets. "I need to work on my game. I need to practice. I don't believe in talent. I believe in hard work."

Shifting coasts prior to the start of the 1996–97 season, Shaq moved from Florida to California, where he signed a staggering $120 million contract to play for the Los Angeles Lakers. Shaq, who was selected as one of the 50 greatest players in NBA history, immediately made his presence felt, leading the team in most major offensive and defensive categories, and helping them reach the Western

Conference semi-finals. "We're asking him to do everything," said Laker coach Del Harris. "To be our leading scorer, our leading rebounder and shot blocker. To beat the opposing big man down the court and draw the defense to him. He deserves to be recognized as a great player because he is a great player."

Shaq came back even stronger the following year, topping the league in field goal percentage and finishing second behind Michael Jordan in the scoring race with a 28.3 average. And despite being forced to sit out 22 games, Shaq was able to come back and lead the Lakers to a 61-21 record and a piece of the Pacific Division title. Shaq raised his level of game still higher in the first two rounds of the postseason, as the Lakers steamrolled past the Portland Trail Blazers and the Seattle SuperSonics. "Shaq was great," admitted Gary Payton, Seattle's All-Star point guard. "We couldn't deal with him. He destroyed us."

But Shaq and his young Laker teammates ran in to a serious roadblock in the Western Conference finals, and were wrecked by the veteran Utah Jazz, 4–0. Even in the ashes of defeat, however, Shaq showed that he had the character and maturity to learn from the loss and use it to build toward future victories.

"Michael Jordan once told me that you have to learn how to fail before you can learn to succeed," said O'Neal, finding a positive purpose in the pain of defeat. "It took Michael seven years to win his first title. If you look at history, that's how long it takes most players. That was my sixth season. I think I've learned. Now, I'm ready to succeed."

SHAQUILLE O'NEAL

Born: March 6, 1972, in Newark, New Jersey
Height: 7' 1"   Weight: 320
College: Louisiana State
Round drafted: First (1992)
NBA seasons: 6

CAREER STATS *(per game average)*

Points	Assists	Rebounds	Steals	Blocks
27.2	2.5	12.3	.80	2.7